UNSTOPPABLE
ARSENAL
FULL METAL SUPERHERO: BOOK 2
BY JEFFERY H. HASKELL

D1521340

For Rebekah, Julia, John, and Rivkah...
This is an Ex-Parrot.

Humans are walking, talking contradictions. Utterly predictable right up until they are not.

-Notes on an Electronic Life, by Epic

Incoming fire. Recommend evasive maneuvers.

"You think?" I ask as I throw myself sideways. Turning at high speeds is like slamming into a wall but I manage to stay conscious. The space I occupied a moment before is filled with 20mm cannon fire. A second later two F-22s, tails painted with the Arizona Air Guard emblem, flash by in a streak of fire and fury.

"Let's see how they climb. Full power to the Emdrive."

We're already at fifteen thousand feet about twenty miles north of Tucson Air Guard base, home of the 162d Air Combat wing. A few weeks ago the governor asked if we would be willing to cross train with the other State militias. Fighting actual jets sounded like fun and since they couldn't hurt me... Also, with the MKI retired after all the acid scoring I needed to do a proper field test of the MKII. I told them to use live weapons. They thought I was joking until I showed them the video of the fifty cals bouncing off my shields. This is our third sortie in four days and I'm loving it. I may have bitten off more than I can chew, but this is the perfect testbed for the Mark II upgrade.

The fighters are coming around. Two are going high to cut you off.

I lock my arms down to stabilize as I blast near straight up.

Their radar is searching.

They won't find anything.

"Epic, lock on the lead jet with the particle beam and inform his computer when he's dead." As soon as my AI comes back with a targeting solution I cut thrust to float for a few seconds. As the g's dissipate I bring my arm up, wrist down and point it where he tells me. I don't actually fire. The beam would slice through the pilot's plane and I don't have seventy-million dollars to replace it.

Splash one.

Epic is really into all the military jargon and I can't say I blame him. I'm dogfighting with— the sky lights up in a shower of flame. A shockwave hits and I'm flailing through the air. My shields scream at me for more power and I can hear the *ping* of debris deflecting off my armor.

"How did we miss that one?"

They took advantage of your momentary lapse in speed to fire a missile at you without locking on. The pilot 'eyeballed' it. Detonation was ten feet behind us.

I kick in the Emdrive and I'm shooting through the air. My airspeed approaches six-hundred and the air starts to condense in front of me as I approach the so-called sound barrier.

"Give me their ears, Epic." A few seconds pass and a green light pop's on my HUD.

"Okay, boys, you got me. Good hit. Now, let's see who can hit sixty-thousand feet the fastest."

The radio distorts his reply, "You heard her, Valkyrie Three—Tally-ho!"

Valkyrie Three and Four surge past about a half mile away. Their tails light a trail in the sky as the engines effortlessly push them past Mach One quickly followed by Mach Two.

"Full burn! Straight up." My HUD flashes as the parts in my improved systems re-arrange themselves to give me maximum thrust from my new drive. All power from my Zero Point Field Module shunts into the Emdrive and a burst of acceleration elicits a grunt from me. Epic locks me up since we're on a ballistic trajectory. The whole thing takes three seconds, but in that time the fighters have shot up seven thousand feet. My airspeed indicator highlights for ease of visual reference.

I don't know what I was expecting when I crossed the sound barrier. I hoped it would be cool. It was just another number on the screen. I'm sure from below it sounds awesome. Three seconds later we hit Mach Two. Next time I do this I need to arrange someone to film it.

"More power!" I really want to beat these guys. Epic flashes the amount of joules he's already dumping into the Emdrive and even I'm impressed. The drive is fantastic but it was never meant for operating in an atmosphere. The idea was designed for space with no friction and a ten-watt battery recharged by solar winds. With a little tweaking and a few hundred-thousand watts it can push me just about anywhere I want to go.

Mach 3.

I let out a *whoop* on the radio as I blast by sixty-thousand feet a half second before the jets.

The radio crackles to life with the pilot's voice, "If you ever want to rent one of those out, ma'am, I know about fifty men and women who would love to take it for a spin," he tells me. He has a nice voice and if I recall correctly, he's an older fellow and the commander of the wing. A colonel?

"That probably won't happen Colonel, but if I ever consider it, I think you would be the man for the job." They squawk their radios as they turn south to head back to base. We're still doing Mach 3 as we just pass eighty thousand feet. The air is thinning. A plane would be slowed by the thinning air as it would receive less lift under the wings... but since I don't rely on aerodynamics to maneuver it has the effect of speeding us up due to the lack of resistance.

"What do you say, Epic? Give the Mark II a spin in space? Be the first non-powered human in orbit without a shuttle?

Not today. There is an emergency call coming in from HQ. All hands on deck. A gang of super-powered criminals known as the 'Riot Boys' are attacking Phoenix.

"Attacking? Just attacking, not robbing anything?"

It is unclear at this time. They have leveled a small building and are blowing up parked cars. Speed is suggested. Fleet is currently on scene evacuating civilians.

"I guess it's time to show off the MK II after all. Bring us about, Number One, and send us on our way."

The trajectory for the course flashes on the HUD as Epic brings us over and kicks in the drive. At our altitude it only takes a few seconds to reach Phoenix.

Wind roars by as we plunge toward the city I've called home most of my life. Excitement builds in my gut as we close the distance. I can't wait to show off my new tech!

"Any update on what they're doing?"

Yes. While their actions appear to be random they are in fact setting up distractions while a small team infiltrates a jewelry outlet in the Paradise Valley area.

Paradise Valley is right next to Glendale and it is the fanciest neighborhood in the city. Which means plenty of cops on scene and possible arguments over jurisdiction. However, if the bad guys are using superpowers then they're ours.

Phoenix in September is a lot like Phoenix in June, hot enough to fry an egg on the outside of my armor. Lucky for me, I have climate control. My heart goes out to the rest of the team who don't. Though Mr. Perfect manages to stay annoyingly sweat free, Kate's body regulates itself so she's never out of place, and Fleet just runs everywhere to cool off. Which just leaves Luke, aka Major Force, out in the heat.

He has some luck today, though. The newest member of the Diamondbacks is finally out of state training and should be joining us. Glacier is little more than a kid at seventeen, but with no ability to turn her powers off, and her life endangered by them, the government decided to allow her family to relocate to

Phoenix so she could join us. Elementals are fairly rare, and ice is the rarest of all, and it will be nice to have one on our side for once.

"Okay, Epic, before we descend why don't you give me the recon. Luke will ask for it as soon as we're on scene anyways."

Affirmative.

Part of me is glad the last three months since the monster attack were quiet. I spent a lot of time in the lab working on my three big upgrades. My Emdrive, the computronium spray over my chest piece, and of course my upgraded grenade launcher. The computronium allows Epic to live in the suit, it is a nano thick layer of a gold-titanium alloy capable of forming computer cores. Once I sprayed the suit with it, connected the components and then sealed it with a quarter inch layer of new armor, it allowed me to upload Epic. Faster than his old housing, and more importantly, with me in the suit. This means I can travel at sixty-thousand feet and not lose contact with him.

Data flashes up on my green HUD. Multiple windows open showing me pictures and video. Fleet, fast as always, grabs civilians and whisks them away to the evac zone, an underground parking garage a mile away. Luke, Kate, Mr. Perfect, and Glacier, are on top of the mall staying out of sight until I arrive. Good for Luke. Sometimes he has trouble remembering tactics.

There are nineteen members of the gang in the street and six in the diamond exchange. Epic flashes the rundown on every known member, almost all of them are F3 with variations of 'fast and strong'. The three we need to watch out for are, Inferno, Crusher, and Fang. Inferno is an elemental of the most common type, flame. Crusher is their strong man, an F4 with mass generation. Ugh, mass is the enemy in a fight. The last, Fang is one of the beast modes. The poor bastards who upon receiving their powers turn into creatures out of nightmares or worse. Sometimes they're recognizable, other times not. Fang is rather tame, like a wolf crossed with a spider that grew fly wings.

Inferno and Crusher are leading the rampant street destruction team, Fang is in charge of the team infiltrating the exchange. I have Epic flash this news to the Diamondbacks. They all wear augmented reality goggles now, Epic can give them updates, directions, show them info about who they're fighting, the whole bit. I spared no expense.

"ETA twenty seconds, boss," I say over the team tacnet.

"Affirmative. Come in stealthy, Domino has a plan," Luke replies.

"Stealth mode." The HUD switches from the ubiquitous green to the soft blue as light levels are lowered. I don't need to worry about sound baffling or thermal energy anymore, the Emdrive puts off neither. Mostly the plates on my armor shift around to a radar friendly configuration. I'm still working on invisibility, but with this and the kinetic emitters rigged for silent running, I'm invisible to radar detection.

I land with a thud on the black tar roof. Heat from the midday sun turns it into a soft goo which sticks to my boots.

"What's the plan?" I ask. My synthesized voice sounds more robotic than me. I find most people respond better to it than to my natural voice, which isn't exactly authoritative.

Kate flashes me a smile, "A reverse on our takedown of the Six. Fleet has the whole area clear of civvies, the guys at the diamond exchange are stuck on the vault, which gives us something we don't normally have," she finishes with a smile.

"A dress code?" Mr. Perfect asks.

"Lunch?" Fleet adds as he zips up to stand perfectly still in a rush of wind.

"Time," I say.

"And the prize goes to the armored heroine," Luke mimes a roaring crowd.

I spy Glacier shaking her head. She'll get used to it. We've been together as a team for almost six months now, and the things we've faced have really brought us together.

"I'll teleport one of them to us, we beat him up, lock him down, and then rinse and repeat until they're a... more manageable size."

It's a good plan.

"Epic switch to stun rounds on the launcher, we're going to want minimal collateral damage here."

Affirmative.

Glacier raises an eyebrow at me as the drum on my back cycles. It was my answer to flexibility on the grenades. I can now carry sixteen grenades and as many types as I want. I still load mostly bean bags and pods. Today I'm also loaded with two high-explosives and a flash-bang.

"Okay everyone," Luke puts his hand out. The smile on his face is worth all the money I've put into the suit. When we first met he was so unhappy. But now... not just the team has come together. We spend an awful lot of our off hours together and I can't help but blush thinking about the hours we whittle away on my couch.

Fleet goes first, then Perfect and Domino, followed by me. We all look to Glacier when her hand doesn't appear.

"This is stupid," she says in a curt, teenage voice.

"Yes," I reply, "It is, but we do it anyway. Now put your hand in."

She does.

"Remember, stop the bad guys, save people, kick their ass. Diamondbacks," Domino cheers.

Everyone except for Glacier chants 'Diamondbacks'. She'll get the hang of it eventually. Teamwork takes time to build and no one adapts overnight.

We spread out in a circle. Kate wants me to have first shot on the ones with few powers or those who have less... useful powers. Glacier is to my right and I can tell she's nervous from the way she rolls her shoulders. Not that she has shoulders. Elementals defy science in a way that is beyond the rest of the super people. Poor Glacier is one of the worst. When her powers expressed her entire body transmuted into living ice. I'm standing right next to her and I can see the light filtering through her arms.

"What?" she snaps at me.

I shake my head. Great Amelia, fantastic. Stare at the person who is different.

"Sorry, I was curious as to how cold your surface temperature would have to maintain in the Arizona heat," I say lamely.

I was, but that wasn't why I gawked at her. In a way, Glacier is beautiful. It is as if someone carved a statue out of ice and imbued it with life. Her hair, eyes, even her fingernails are all there exactly as they should be, just ice.

"What are you, another scientist? Just stay out of my business." She waves her hand in my face, "I have enough problems without more poking and prodding."

"First in three... two..." Kate's voice interrupts us... or saves me, I'm not sure which.

There is a pop and standing on the roof is Kate with her hands holding onto a man whose eyes couldn't get any bigger. It takes his brain a half second to process what happened before he drops to his knees and throws his hands up.

"Smart boy," Luke rumbles as he clamps on the plus-sized manacles.

Luke drags him to the side making room for Fleet. Kate can't teleport twenty times in a row without exhausting herself. This was the test run. Fleet disappears in a blur and is back a half second later with a guy who looks like he stepped out of an old movie. He's wearing distressed leather everything, boots, pants, vest and a beard that runs to his exposed beer belly.

He swings a backhand at Fleet, who dodges the blow with ease. Epic fires the bean bag at the thug with enough force to break bones. It hits him square in the gut, sending him doubling over and moaning. Then Luke is there restraining him and it's done. *Two down... seventeen to go.*

Three more go by quick. Fleet focuses on the low-powered ones, thanks to his AR goggles he knows who is who. Lucky number seven screws us up.

Fleet appears, dropping someone barely older than me in the circle. The kid is scrawny, baggy clothing, sunken cheekbones, and stringy hair. Perhaps the last three were too easy, but I don't tag him as fast as I should because he's a kid.

He opens his mouth to say something, but it comes out a scream. Sonic waves emanate from him in such decibels that even the sound dampeners on my helmet short out. The roof explodes in a shockwave. I'm sailing through the air with a nice view of the Arizona sun and a ringing in my ears that isn't going away anytime soon.

There is absolutely no way the rest of the Riot boys didn't hear that.

The kid is flying. Not only that, he has Luke on his knees with his sonic voice. Blood seeps from my man's ears and the roof under his knees crumples. *Up Amelia!*

I'm now thankful I kept Epic as an on-screen presence because I can't hear a damn thing.

"IP Cannon, full power, narrow beam," I say hoping Epic can hear me through the cacophony.

Arms forward, palms up, I yell for Epic to fire. It is like being in a silent film; I can't even hear myself scream just a high pitched ringing in my ears and a hollow tone behind it. The ionic pulse energy strikes out at the teen, catching him in the shoulder. The energy transfer flings him twenty feet away to crash into the quickly disintegrating rooftop.

He isn't listed as having this power, but he is in the database.

That's weird, but I don't have time to ponder it. The remaining thirteen 'Riot Boys', which is a stupid name since some of them are girls, are coming for us. I still can't hear, and if it's this bad for me I can only imagine how bad it is for everyone else.

"Epic. Thrusters. Give us some altitude, switch to pods and go to automatic fire."

As we climb I feel the slight vibration of the grenade launcher and see the counter rapidly descend as my computer sidekick fires off the eight AG Pods I have and the four other bean bags leaving me with only the two high explosives and the flashbang.

Out of twelve shots, six incapacitate or remove combatants from the field. All of a sudden they go from thirteen to seven. Lucky number seven, again.

I smile at myself for a job well done. Unfortunately, with the pods exhausted, and half the Riot Boys and Girls (I've decided to rename them) floating off into the atmosphere, all I'm left with are my IP cannons, Kinetic Lance, and two very, very deadly options.

Domino and Luke are taking on three of them at once, each punching, jumping, and dodging in a ballet as beautiful as it is deadly. Luke is a marvel of a man. As his adrenaline pumps, he grows in size from an already impressive six-four to six-eight. His mass increases too while not inhibiting his nimbleness at all if anything it increases. He dodges blows he can't possibly see coming and lands counter punches at angles no one can hope to block. He loses his mind though, which is the downside. He runs purely on instinct and anger when he's like this.

Domino, while not as kinetic or strong as Luke, has her own grace and beauty. She teleports around her opponents. Punching them from odd angles and kicking them when they are looking the other way. She uses a variety of weapons from Tazers, to zip ties in a Jackie Chan-esq ballet of incapacitation.

Fleet zooms around slapping his opponents with debris and shoving them into walls. He can't punch anyone at speed without breaking every bone in his body. I can only imagine how careful he has to be. His friction field protects him to some degree, but not from punching a human at a hundred miles an hour. However, even a pebble causes serious harm if it's going fast enough.

Mr. Perfect has several contained in one of his energy constructs, a box that shrinks in size by the second. He does all of this from his flying carpet while chanting and waving his hands... goofball.

I look for Glacier to make sure she is okay and... I can't find her.

"Epic, locate Glacier."

He flashes a search pattern on my HUD before it zeroes in on her. She is sliding south down the road toward the Diamond Exchange. Great, she wants to go solo against Fang. I glance around the struggle before me. Crusher and Inferno vanished the moment the fight broke out. Which means the team can handle these losers.

Either Glacier is aching to prove herself or she wants to get hurt. On the bright side, I can hear again.

"Boss, permission to engage the DE with Glacier?" I ask Luke. "It looks like Inferno and Crusher are a no-show."

He kicks one of the gang members in the chest, sending him flying backward end over end to crash into a car. The door crumples and the man doesn't get up. The car is one of those cheaply built electric jobs that cost an arm and a leg. Which we're now going to have to pay for.

"Affirmative. Keep her out of trouble," Luke replies.

I turn south and kick in the speed. I miss the roar my compressed fuel jets used to make. Glacier travels by freezing the ground in front of her with a thick sheet of ice, then sliding on it. She must have phenomenal balance. Once she gets going she really moves. I have floor it to catch up.

"Nice afternoon for a skate?"

The huge advantage of my new suit is the Emdrive allows me to hover without having to use my hands for balance. I can fly along at twenty-five miles an hour simply by angling myself up and letting my new maneuvering thrusters do the rest.

"You," she sighs, "Can't I do my own thing? I don't need a babysitter."

"As a matter of fact, as a probationary member, you *do* need a babysitter. Everyone gets one until they're a full-fledged member, that means you. What are you doing?"

She shrugs.

"The way my... abilities work, I don't like to use them around people I don't want frozen," she says as we approach the front entrance of the diamond exchange.

I read her file, she can flash freeze things but she can also rapidly build ice up around herself and others.

Not to mention the tricks she can do with it, like ice skating when it's ninety-five out.

"Epic, could we generate enough heat to melt ice if we were incased?"

Other than the minimal amount of life-support required for our eventual crack at orbital flight—no. I wouldn't recommend being frozen.

"Thanks..." Don't get frozen, right.

The Diamond Exchanges outer doors are the kind of roll down metal slats business use to protect themselves from vandals. These didn't help at all, someone peeled them back like bananas.

"What is Fang's strength rated at?"

F4 and his claws are sharp enough to shred metal.

It was a good choice of words on Epic's part, considering the next set of doors were made of reinforced steel. Fang went through them like a can opener.

"Be ready for anything," I say to Glacier.

Epic throws up some telemetry on my HUD. Heat sources, sound, etc. I notice he's picking up vitals from Glacier. I'll have to ask him about that later.

With palms toward the door, I land the suit and start in. Glacier is right behind me. She's not tall, only five-six, which is funny because if I could stand that would be my height. In the suit, though, I'm five-eight and much bulkier than a normal person.

With the power out, I turn on the suits exterior LED's, they're bright enough to light up the dark side of the moon. There isn't a lot of natural light in here. Fewer windows mean fewer entrances to guard, I guess.

Movement. Up ahead, three meters.

"That's in the room..."

An invisible wall of force slams into me, sending me flying backward. Glacier narrowly dodges and I see her hands shoot out. Beams of blue light flash through the empty air leaving behind splashes of ice wherever they touch.

I hear a scream as I pull myself back up. A man appears out of thin air and drops to the floor, holding his frozen hand. I try not to think about it as I zap him with an IP cannon blast. He falls to the ground convulsing as his nervous system short-circuits.

Glacier chuckles.

"Cool weapon."

"Invisi-dork must be the rear guard. They probably know we're here, be careful."

I don't wait for her to respond before I start moving again. She didn't panic which says a lot about her.

"Arsenal, this is Force." As if I don't know what he sounds like. "We're all cleaned up out here and moving toward you. The two ring-leaders are a no-show."

I nod to myself. Something fishy is going on here but I'm not sure what.

"Roger Dodger, meet us around back, maybe we can flush some of these guys out to you?"

The Exchange is essentially a big warehouse with cages for buying and selling precious gems. On one side they have the massive vaults and in the middle, the showroom. When we enter the open area the remaining four members of the team are busy looting one of the vaults that look like it was peeled open.

"Glacier," I whisper, "Freeze the floor."

"All of it?"

I give her the thumbs up as I take to the air. Her hands go out in front of her and the blue light flashes from her palms. Wherever she shines the light a thick layer of ice grows behind it. The room is instantly more humid from the sudden influx of frozen h2o.

"Attention bad guys," I say at a hundred decibels, "You are under arrest for the crime of being stupid. Give up now and we may reconsider the charges."

When I first started doing this I thought I sounded hokey, until I heard Luke talk.

The four gang members stop what they are doing and look back to me. I don't expect them to throw their hands up but pointing and laughing weren't high on my list either.

"Okay, have it your way," I say aloud, then to Epic, "IP Cannons, maxi—"

The suit bucks as something hits me. The Emdrive flashes red as my apparent weight has... no, he's on my back. Thick spider-like legs covered in fine wolf's fur wrap around me. Epic diverts full power to the kinetic dampeners as the thing holding me spins me around while... ew, covering me in webs. Gross.

"Particle cannons," I yell as I spin. Epic flashes a three-dimensional schematic of the room on my HUD. With my arms trapped at my side, I need to be careful not to shoot Glacier. Fang is a lot like a real spider, he finishes wrapping me one way then spins me around to start the other direction. However, as he spins me—I fire.

Super accelerated silicon particles slice through his webbing and parts of him. He howls and drops me thirty feet to the floor. The suit bounces after it hits and I land face down.

Of course.

I can activate my thrusters but thanks to my upgrade they don't produce any flame. I can't burst the stuff because I'm not strong enough. That just leaves...

"Epic, unlock the sword."

Without the kinetic field holding my four-foot long black blade to my back, there's nothing stopping it from falling. Even a tiny bit of gravity can cause it to shift. With the edge being one molecule thick of diamond, all it has to do is touch the fibers and it slices between their bonds like they aren't even there!

A few seconds more and I can move. I snatch up the sword then carefully slice through the webbing around my legs. Once I'm free, I can stand. The four gang members have split into two groups, one continues to load the backpacks while the other two go after Glacier. Arrogant dorks that they are, they don't even notice Fang retreating. I can't say I blame him. The leg I cut off is still twitching on the floor.

The two attacking Glacier have her pinned. One is shooting some kind of focused energy beams from his eyes, while the other leaps around her like a frog on crack.

"Epic, HE in the vault when the two guys aren't in it."

I whip my sword around a few times to shake the cobwebs off of it before clicking it into place. It's just too deadly to use on flesh and blood people.

I hear the *puff* of the grenade launcher. Two seconds later the explosion rips through the vault with a deafening boom. IP Cannon's nail leaper when he's distracted. The energy slams him thirty feet into the far wall as if he were weightless.

Interesting.

I miss eye-beam-man and bring my hand around to refocus. Alarms sound and my HUD flashes red. Heat levels rise as the outside temperature of the armor begins to climb. He's focused on me, the red beam burns through the air striking the side of the armor. At the rate the temperature's climbing I have thirty seconds until the titanium-tungsten carbide outer shell softens.

Too bad he doesn't have that long.

"IP cannons, maximum power, narrow beam."

The targeting bracket hovers over him showing me exactly where my twin IP cannons will strike. Since he's not moving because of the ice I take an extra second to make sure I'll get a headshot.

The sandpaper sound of my cannons discharging fills the air. The two force blasts strike him in the face shattering his nose and sending him sprawling backward head over feet sliding on the floor until he bumps unconscious against the far wall.

"Wow," Glacier says as she moves beside me.

"Careful, my armor is about a thousand degrees right now." It will take a good hour for the armor to cool off. I sigh. This is going to take a hundred hours of maintenance and diagnostics to make sure nothing was damaged.

"I got it," she says. She lifts her hand up to my chest piece and the temperature drops rapidly. Not instantly, not fast enough to damage it, but about twice as long as it took to heat up.

"Wow," I say.

She shrugs.

"Part of being an ice elemental is the constant need to absorb heat. If I don't absorb enough then..."

"What?" I ask.

"I freeze in place," she says looking down at the ground. I can tell this is upsetting her so I switch lines.

"You held your own against leaping lizard and gazer beam over there, good job."

She looks up and a smile splits her icy face. I still can't get over how ice can move and react exactly like a person but not be one. I mean, I can see through her head. She is a walking, talking statue of ice...

So how come Epic can detect a heartbeat?

O nly after I land the suit down in my workshop do I feel tired. The day started almost twelve hours ago and my arms feel like jelly. I take a step over to my right, lining up my oversized boots with the taped out squares on the floor. I keep meaning to turn them into something more permanent, but if it ain't broke...

Epic takes over and the suit shifts. While the MKI used the kinetic manipulators to detach and form, I decided with the MKII I needed a way to take the suit with me. I never want to be in the position again of having to rely on outwitting someone like Vixen who sneaks into my lab. Of course, taking the suit off and on isn't something I can do by hand, so I had to get clever.

Each piece of the suit slides down as the plates shift and reform. It only takes thirty seconds but when it's done I'm sitting in a shiny red and white wheelchair with hi-tech looking wheels. The chair isn't formed from the armor, more of a storage unit for it. I can press a button and be in the suit in a few seconds, but I can only repackage and take it off, here in the lab.

I also bit the bullet and motorized it, though I try really hard to use my arms whenever I can. Upper body strength is crucial for building and operating the suit. As much as I like walking around in the suit, it isn't real. The suit does the work and my legs are just along for the ride. Though, a nice added benefit from wearing it is the physical therapy of keeping my paralyzed parts moving.

"Arsenal, Force here. The AG would like a debrief on the Riot Boys asap," Luke says over the comms.

Sigh. I was so looking forward to a long shower and a nap. I grab a Coke from the fridge, Doritos, and a Snickers and I am on my way. I haven't eaten all day and my blood sugar has got to be rock bottom. Something I need to fix if I'm still going to go through with my extracurricular activity tonight. I slip my augmented reality glasses out of the chair and slide them on so I can interact with Epic. They're a stylish pair, more like fancy prescription glasses than the work goggles I'd made before. Except these have a slight yellow tint to help with contrast in the bright sun.

"Epic, run a full diagnostics and make sure we are up to snuff for our little trip. Also, make a note, we need to add a Camelback to the suit or something. Someway to take some form of nourishment with us."

Affirmative. I will add 'soda dispenser' to our project list. Enjoy your meeting.

"You know me too well."

The team's offices take up the second floor, the third and fourth are the workout, training, and conference rooms, and the first floor is the lobby and museum. Which, up until six months ago, didn't have a lot in it.

After we took down The Creature we experienced an influx of traffic. Luckily, it has died down since then. While the Arizona government, my team, and Cat-7 know my identity, I would rather it wasn't public. Having civilians wondering around our HQ compromises that. I already have Epic combing the Internet for signs that my identity has been leaked. If he finds any he'll wipe them out.

It's weird being the object of so much admiration. We still see a dozen people a day coming and going looking at the tourist part of our little brick building.

As I roll into the briefing I hear the AG's voice. Crap, I'm late. Oh well. I wheel in with my soda between my legs and my bag of Doritos clenched in my mouth. He's just gonna have to deal. Sometime between returning to base and now Luke managed a shower, I can smell the old spice on him and it warms my stomach. I knew I shouldn't have spent a half hour flying around Phoenix looking for the missing leadership. I very much don't smell freshly showered.

I shiver as I roll up to the table, I have my own spot they keep clear of chairs, and Luke even lowered the height so I didn't look like the kid trying to eat at the adult table at Thanksgiving. Glacier or I guess Monica since we are 'off duty', is across the table from me. She's wearing a parka, which seems weird but then she has to keep warm or she will freeze solid. Still, just having her in here lowers the ambient temperature by twenty degrees. Should be good for our AC bill.

"Thank you for joining us Arsenal," the AG says from the giant flat screen on the wall. He's smiling so he can't be too upset.

I smile back, "Sorry sir it takes a few seconds to get the armor off..."

Luke reaches over and touches my hand under the table. It is about as public a show of affection as he's capable of.

"I'm disappointed you weren't able to capture the leaders of the gang, but regardless. Having sixteen members off the streets is pretty impressive."

I pop the top on my soda and freeze as everyone glances my way.

"Sorry," I say, taking a long drink.

"They weren't so much as not captured as they weren't even there. Other than Fang, the leaders were a no-show. Any intel on where they might be?" Luke asks.

The AG, an older man with balding hair and a well-groomed mustache shakes his head.

"No. Is there anything else to report?"

I raise my hand as I take a bite of my Snickers.

"Ms. Lockheart?"

I hold up one finger. Why oh why did I take a bite right before asking a question?

"Any idea—" I swallow, "—why several members of the gang had superpowers that weren't in the database?"

He shakes his head and I can see a trace of a smile on his face. He's a nice man, I've met him once before in person and he's always been very respectful.

"We're looking into the integrity of our local databases but we get all our info from the national ones. If there is a problem with the intel it is likely on a national level. Our DMHA liaison is looking into it."

"Well that isn't reassuring at all," I say as I tear into my Doritos with a loud crunch.

"Job well done, Diamondbacks, enjoy the rest of your day."

There is a chorus of 'thank you' as he signs off. Everyone but Monica smiles and starts talking about the day's adventure. I try to catch Kate's eye but she's busy chatting with Mr. Perfect. Instead, I wheel myself over to the cold girl and park next to her.

"Hi," I say as I chow down on the last of my candy bar, "Want a chip?"

She shakes her head. "I'm sorry I got on you for staring, I forgot..."

I hold out my hand to forestall the apology.

"Me being in a wheelchair doesn't excuse my own rudeness. I'm sorry Monica, I let my fascination with the science behind you override my common sense. I won't let it happen again."

I hold the bag of chips out to her again. Her eyes are like perfectly blue like old ice.

"I... I don't eat," she says, pointing at her stomach, "despite the fact that I look like a person, nothing in here is actually real. According to the Cat-7 doctors, I am held together by will alone."

I nod. I'd read her file, but I trust Cat-7 about as far as I can throw them... out of armor of course.

"I can't say I can do anything, but if you ever want to give me a shot I would love to run some tests. I picked up some odd readings while we were in the field and it gave me an idea."

She raises an eyebrow at me, "What do you mean 'do anything'? Believe me, I've had enough tests to see what I can do, I don't need anymore," her demeanor switches to match her outside, cold. Didn't Cat-7 try to fix her? No... of course they didn't. They just wanted to know how she could be best used as a weapon. I make a mental note to have Epic look for info on her *tests*.

"I am going to go out on a limb and say Cat-7 never even talked to you about the possibility of reversing your transformation?"

Monica goes still as a corpse. Frost spreads quietly out around her hand on the table.

"Don't joke with me Amelia, it isn't funny."

I shake my head, "I never joke about science... in the morning on," I turn to Kate, "What day is it?"

"Tuesday," she says with a raised eyebrow.

"On Tuesday. Not ever."

She cracks a smile and nods, "I'll come by sometime then. Maybe."

"No rush, like I said, I can't promise anything but I wouldn't mind a shot at trying."

She stands up, cold air eddies around her and little bits of frost fall from her like snow.

"Maybe I will, thanks."

I watch her leave and my heart goes out to her. I'm stuck in a chair but I still get to eat, drink, sleep. I still get to feel the warmth of companionship, the kiss of another human being. What does she get? More ice.

"That was sweet, what you said. But careful, I don't know about her emotional state," Kate says stepping up behind me and pushing on my chair.

"My powers have no influence on her. I can read her emotions slightly better than a non-empath can, but as for influence," she shrugs, "I have none."

"Understood. Where are we going?" I ask.

"To get you some real food. Soda and chips doesn't a meal make."

"Clearly you've never played *Battlefield* all night long."

The alarm, high-pitched and shrill, goes off and I immediately slap it. I haven't slept. I wish I had but I'm too... something. Nervous, eager, excited, scared...? Pick one. After fourteen years I will finally have my parents back.

I showered and cleaned up after today's events but I went to sleep in my synthsuit. It isn't uncomfortable and it certainly speeds the process up if I am already dressed. It's easy enough to slide into the chair and wheel over to the marks on the floor. I glance up at the monitor to make sure Epic is ready. He did a full diagnostics with no hiccups.

"Epic, how's Artemis coming along?"

He changes screens and shows my new baby. I'm constantly thinking up things, my mind is a raging inferno of ideas and often times simply writing them out or slapping some blueprints down will do the trick. This one, though, wouldn't leave me alone.

On the screen is the launch site for *Blue Origin*, it's a private space agency founded by the second richest person in the world. When I first had the idea for Artemis I thought it would be impossible to launch my own satellite. Here it is, however, two months and three million dollars later, and she is only a few hours away from launch.

Technically she's a private communications satellite for Mars Tech Global. Blue Origin will put her in geostationary orbit above the equator with a direct line-of-sight to North America. Along with the cost of the launch, I have to pay transponder fees and orbital *rent* to the US government. What they don't know is she's far more than a comsat.

Now that I know she is safe and about to launch I refocus. Time to put an end to my quest.

"Epic... *initiate!*"

I never quite liked the old way the suit came together around me. This is much better. The chair stands me up as plates slide into place. My helmet flips over my head as the HUD boots up and with ten seconds I am fully functional and ready to go.

"Open the window," I order. If I go to the roof there is a chance one of the other team might see me if they are still here. I don't want anyone knowing what I'm doing. I know they would help and I love them for it, especially Luke. But what I am about to do is illegal and dangerous and my responsibility.

The Emdrive kicks in and I shoot out into the night sky. I love how silent the new propulsion is, barely more than a hum at full power. Ten thousand feet pass in the blink of an eye as I approach the speed of sound. There is something about the roar of jets that is exhilarating, but the advantages of stealth and speed of the Emdrive far outweigh hearing the sound. Besides, jet fuel was expensive and the process to compress it was inherently dangerous.

"Course plotted?"

Plotted.

I've always wanted to say this… "Punch it!"

The suit locks up and the drive goes to full power mode. The wind buffets the suit like mad and the closer I get to Mach One the worse it is. Thank goodness I'm just a passenger. I imagine the boom in my head as the readout passes Mach One followed a few seconds later by two, then three. As we approach eighty-thousand feet and Mach Four Epic evens out our trajectory. With

Arizona air being dry as it is I don't leave a vapor trail or a shock cone.

No Orbit today.

"I know, not the mission. ETA?"

37 minutes.

"Show me the most recent footage?"

A window opens up on the HUD. The camera angle is an ATM across the street. A few other windows open up with red light camera footage, CCTV and even a few pictures posted on the Internet. Part of why I want Artemis is if I have to do anything like this in the future, I want my own spy satellite.

Then it hits me... will I do this in the future? With Mom and Dad back there won't be a need for Arsenal anymore. A hollow pit forms in my stomach. Clearly, I didn't give this any advance thought. To this point, my life has been about finding out what happened to my parents and saving them if I could. Here I am on the cusp of doing so and...

Amelia, I am detecting elevated heart rate and respiratory duress. Are you okay?

"Minor panic attack, buddy. Just thinking about the future and my place in it."

To be or not to be, is that the question?

"Ha. I guess so."

A new window opens and washes all the others away. The opening bars of Star Wars start and I am instantly more relaxed. Epic's ability to read my emotional state and help me through trials is borderline unbelievable.

Thirty minutes later, and a daring escape from Tatooine, I'm closing in on Boston. It's six a.m. local so the city is waking up and coming alive with activity. Though, I don't think this city ever truly stops. The place I'm looking for is near the harbor off of Dorchester Street. A big white warehouse with no signs, just a chain link fence, and the standard *private property stay out* message. Epic highlights the location on the HUD as we come down toward the city. At twenty thousand feet he cuts the thrusters and I'm free falling.

Wind rushes around me as I dive toward the ground. The airspeed indicator on my HUD slows down as friction and atmospheric density drag me toward terminal velocity, which is quite a bit slower than Mach Four.

"Stealth mode," I tell him.

The HUD switches to soft blue. Radar signature, ECM, and thermals all pop up replacing speed and altitude. With JFK airport nearby there are tons of signals flying around. Epic reconfigures my kinetic shields to disperse the radar waves, making my already small cross signature non-existent.

I am detecting quantum radiation ahead. It appears this is the correct place.

I don't have an official name for it, but my Zero-Point Field Module gives off a radiation that doesn't exist. It doesn't fall into any bands from alpha to x-ray that I can quantify, and believe me, I've tried. Epic coined the idea of Quantum Radiation and we've been using it ever since. As far as I can tell it is harmless to biological tissue. All Zero-Point energy units give it off. However, the half-life is brief and it decays rapidly. Which makes tracking it problematic. The only reason I even know it exists is the base under Portland. If Cat7 hadn't shown me the ZPFM they had I would never have gotten mine working.

But they did.

I grin as we pass five thousand feet. We're now falling round seventy meters per second.

"Deploy flaps."

I put my hands up and let my knees bend. The shoulder units flip up and panels all over the suit lock open to create as much drag as possible slowing me even further. If radar does see me I need to look like a bird diving or something. Coming in hot at 2,000 miles per hour will turn far too many heads and alert the enemy to my presence.

Two-thousand feet.

"Zoom in on the warehouse, please."

The optics in the suit flash as they click over to a digitally enhanced view. I wish I could have real optics, but there isn't a way to have a telescope in my helmet. However, with an AI manning the electronic enhancements I get a pretty clear view of the warehouse.

"The roof looks like aluminum but the way the light reflects off of it is a little weird. Anything on passive?"

We've got about thirty more seconds until we hit and I need to decide what to do. Land elsewhere and watch? Or go full bore.

"You know what? I've waited long enough. Kinetic shields to full strength, we're going right through the roof."

Affirmative.

Without knowing what it's made of, this could be a little risky, but even if I hit the ground flat the shields will absorb at least ninety percent of the impact.

This doesn't ease my mind as the roof looms larger in my field of view.

"Stealth mode off, prepare for combat."

The HUD flashes red and all my weapon and defensive systems go to full power.

The roof shatters under the impact. I crash through a few feet of rafters before I'm in open air again, only to slam into a concrete slab a few seconds later. I bend at the knees to absorb what little impact there is. The shields worked beautifully.

The only problem is, the place is empty.

"Full scan, make sure you hit the walls with the IR."

Roger.

The warehouse is easily four times the square footage of our HQ. Something about it...

"For a place that looks well-used, shouldn't there be, you know, boxes or something?"

The place is empty. Not only are there no crates, there's no office or holding area just a big empty room.

Rather than stand still and be an easy target I stride toward the back where I think an elevator should be. Maybe they've got a hidden...

Four loud pops echo in the cavernous room behind me. I spin to face whoever just teleported in. Vaguely humanoid in shape, I'm face to face with four honest-to-god robots. Their left arms end in cannons with the same funky thermal reading as the plasma guns from Tucson. I knew the Cabal and Cat-7 were the same.

Amelia, they are powering weapons.

"Right, thrusters on full!"

I soar up as balls of green plasma burn through the air where I was moments before. I line up the far one with my particle beam reticule and fire. Hyper-accelerated silica flashes through the air in a blue beam to splash against the hide of the 'bot. For a second I think it isn't going to work... then the beam bursts through the outer skin and the robot explodes in a shower of debris and parts.

"Scan these things," I yell as I roll hard over.

Scanning.

I don't have a ton of room to maneuver and I certainly don't want to take the fight out on the streets. All I need would be for the 'Sons of Liberty' to show up and then I would have to explain why I was in Massachusetts trespassing on private property. It might be unavoidable though, each time the 'bots miss they vaporize another section of the wall.

I fire another particle beam, cutting off the non-plasma arm of a bot. It doesn't seem to notice but I can tell they are engaging in defensive routines. Their speed is picking up. I snap fire my secondary beam and the particles slices through the wall and I pray I didn't just cut someone in half.

"Okay, no more range weapons and let's assume they're immune to the IP cannons."

I reach over my shoulder and grasp the hilt of my sword. The blade comes free as I dive down toward another. The plasma guns have a six-second recharge window and they seem to explode on whatever solid item they hit first. Keeping the bot in front of me, in the same line as the others, allows me to land for a second and engage with my blade... assuming they won't kill each other.

I step forward and swing my sword up from the side. The diamond-coated blade cuts cleanly through the 'bots chest cavity, revealing the internal workings. A mix of fluids, gel packs, and optic circuitry. Whatever these things are they're advanced.

With their compatriot disabled the other two open fire. I grab the top half of the 'bot I just slaughtered and toss it at the looming balls of plasma. The 'bot is vaporized along with the plasma stream.

Move!

I count in my head as I run toward the first one. I get to three when I cut off its arm, spin and lop off the head unit. I don't know if I will ever build a robot, but I won't make it look human, too easy to destroy.

One.

"Full burn!"

The suit leaps into the air just as the ball of plasma vaporizes the space I cleared.

"Ramming speed!"

We swoop down, scraping the concrete as the suit crashes into the last robot at a hundred miles an hour. The human hand reaches for my head and pushes me back with surprising strength.

"Kinetic lance," I yell as I push the thing down into the ground.

The hand explodes from the impact of kinetic energy. We slide to a halt as the bot struggles to line up its cannon. I manage to stand, put a foot on the plasma arm and ram the sword down the center of its chest. The thing dies slowly and powers down.

"Epic, where the heck did they come from?

Scanning. While it is impossible to detect quantum teleportation I can say with ninety percent accuracy it was used from somewhere below.

"Based on the Portland base, how far down?"

Clever. Calculating.

While Epic calculates I use my eyes to flip through the screens on my HUD. As I thought, the fight drew attention and the Sons of Liberty are on the way.

The Portland base is seventy-five feet below the surface. The building on top of the base is a maintenance facility housing parts and equipment.

"Okay, reroute power to the particle beams. You're going to need at least two point one megawatts to each, can we do that?"

That exceeds the maximum power the particle beams were designed for... I don't advise it.

"No risk, no reward. This is my parents, Epic. If we don't succeed today we will never find them."

Power rerouted.

Based on the Portland base I move to the center of the warehouse. With my legs shoulder width apart, I point my arms straight down.

"Here we go."

I flex my arms, firing off the beams. The heat level in the suit immediately spikes. Normally the beams are active for a maximum of three seconds. The power capacitors and heat exchangers are designed around brief spikes of heat. Even when I added the second beam on my other arm I didn't think about using them as a cutting tool.

Eight seconds pass. Epic puts the local news and police band on the HUD. They are only seconds away.

The hyper-accelerated silica particles burn through the floor vaporizing concrete as they stab down. I'm hoping there will be an air pressure—

Penetration. Fifty feet down, rotate at a rate of ten degrees every six seconds.

Epic draws the pattern over my HUD so I can see exactly how I need to turn. I manage to spin in a circle at almost the right rate. The floor begins to glow red as the concrete heats up. The temperature master alarm flips into pre-warning mode and my HUD flashes a bright orange, letting me know the external temp is reaching dangerous levels.

Three-thousand degrees is the max the suit can take. With the way titanium and tungsten interacts, there is no give. Two thousand nine hundred and ninety-nine, I'm fine, three thousand and the suit melts. I've got the master alarm setup to warn me in five hundred degree increments. At twenty-five hundred the suit screams at me.

Ten more seconds.

We can't make it, I was hoping to burn a hole through the ceiling but the heat level is climbing too fast and the Boston PD is almost here.

"Epic, change of plans," I shut down the particle beams with a hundred degrees to spare. "Scan the building for network cables..."

Northwest corner.

I kick in the thrusters and we're there in a second. I punch a hole in the metal box and rip off the door. Inside, there are about a hundred cables. I press my hands up to the master switch. Normally I have Epic break into a wireless network. However, when that isn't possible he can interact with the magnetic field of wires if there's physical contact. "Epic, scan their network for the quantum teleporter and get us in there!" I can hear sirens now, along with the approaching whine of hoverbikes.

I'm in. Hacking. Their security protocols are incredibly advanced. Five seconds.

"Smoke!"

Two compressed canisters of potassium chlorate and aluminum coated fiberglass explode outward from each hip, spewing purple smoke behind me. The room quickly fills with the obscuring screen. I'm gonna have to scrub the suit when I get home, that stuff doesn't come out easy.

System secured, activating quantum teleportation. Hold on to your lunch.

The world goes wonky. My vision *bends* as the wall in front of me vanishes and I am standing in a room with six circular pads. I drop to one knee and almost have to open the faceplate to vomit. I manage to choke it down with a few gasping breaths.

"Why was—" I gulp a few times, "Why was that so disorienting?"

Unknown.

"You're helpful."

I believe you mispronounced, "Thank you Epic for saving me."

"Everyone's a critic," I say as I stand... I don't believe it.

"Epic is this a... a transporter room?"

Yes.

There are six white pads on the floor in a circle and a console not ten feet away with the controls for the quantum teleporter. If I didn't know better I would think I walked onto the set of a Star Trek movie.

"Okay, full active sensors. There's no hiding our presence and I want to be ready."

He doesn't answer but I see the response on the HUD as every bit of ECM we have goes live. The door slides open and two men rush in, they're wearing technician's coats and carrying laptops. They freeze when they see me.

I don't. IP cannons sing their sandpaper staccato, filling the techs with ionic energy and leaving them spazzing on the ground. Okay, now I smile.

"Let's find my parents."

The base isn't nearly as big as Portland, no five-star restaurant, entertainment room, or other amenities.

So far I've found a barebone barracks with incredibly spartan arrangements, a few apartments and a cafeteria that looks like prison food would be a step up. We've run into at least twenty people, all technicians, no guards, and I've stunned them all.

"You get through their wireless firewall yet?"

It is incredibly advanced and the coding is dense. The algorithm I'm building to break it will take time. Amelia, whoever designed this understands how AIs work. I wouldn't be surprised if we encounter one in the near future.

Awesome. How do I design defensive protocols against AIs? The advantage Epic has over traditional firewalls in incalculable. There isn't a network in the world he can't access given enough time. The only trade-off is staying undetected or not.

"Epic make a note on this. We're going to have to put in some serious brain trust time, maybe Mom can help? Her notes were what I used to finish you."

Take the next right.

"You're in?"

Negative. Audio sensors detect the sound of shredding paper.

I hear it now. The double doors are marked *restricted*. Psh. The IP cannon makes short work of them, blowing the right door off its hinges and leaving it hanging awkwardly. I kick it aside as I step through. It is a lab alright. A dozen people are in here and from the looks of it, they're busy wiping hard drives and shredding documents.

I stun the two nearest ones and pass their twitching bodies.

"Special delivery, one angry daughter missing her parents..."

Very Funny, Epic says.

I thought so. My head bounces as a pipe clangs off my helmet.

"Seriously?" I say aloud.

I send a tech sprawling with a blast from a cannon.

"Would John and Hope Lockheart please come forward, I'm here to rescue you," I say with a grin. One of the remaining nine has to be them but they all have their backs to me... and it has been so long that...

He turns around.

Dad.

I want to run to him and hug him but they don't know who I am. Now, where's...

She's right next to him. They're older than I remember, fourteen years is a long time. He's almost forty-three now and she's thirty-eight. He still has the same round nose I remember. His once brown hair is speckled with gray.

Mom's raven black hair is shorter than I remember, but it's my mom. I'll never forget their faces. All of a sudden I am six years old again, riding in the back of the car.

"That's us. Please don't hurt anyone else," he says.

"I'm not here to hurt anyone, I'm here to rescue you!"

They look at each other and I see confusion in their expressions.

"Rescue us? What kind of trick is this? We work here, we're not—"

I don't know what's going on but I have to show them.

"Retract faceplate."

The silver opaque shield over my face retracts, "Mom, Dad, it's me, Amelia," I walk forward and he grabs Mom by the waist and pulls her tight.

I stop. They're not emaciated but not healthy either. In fact, no one I've seen so far could be accused of being well fed. My vision narrows at the abuse they must have suffered.

"I— I don't know who you are but please don't hurt my wife."

Don't know... my heart pounds and I can't breathe. How do they not know who I am?

"I'm your daughter. It's me, Amelia, your daughter. I've been searching for you for fourteen years! How do you not know me?"

He shakes his head and they both are looking at me like I'm crazy, "We never had children. I'm sorry you must be confused. Can you please go and leave us alone? We are doing important work here."

"Important work? Category Seven *kidnapped* you, *stole* you from my life. Epic," I don't bother with lowering the faceplate. "Electromagnetic pulse, full power."

A whine emits from the suit as the capacitor builds up. This is something I've worked on for a while. Whatever is going on here, I am going to destroy this whole lab and leave Cat-7 with nothing.

"Faceplate down." It slides shut. "I don't know why you can't remember me, but you're coming with me. I'm really sorry about this."

"Sorry about—"

"Wide angle IP cannons, fire." I raise my hands and stun everyone in the lab at once. They lose power when I use such a wide angle, but for normal humans, it doesn't make a difference. My parents fall down, twitching but still holding each other. I know that being six when they were taken doesn't leave me with a lot of memories of them, but I remember how much they loved each other. This is them, but how do I get us out?

EMP at the ready.

"Have you broken their wireless yet?"

Their firewall is down, I'm in.

"How much data on their network?"

Hundreds of terabytes. It would take me a day to scan through it all let alone download it.

Dammit, I was hoping to take some files with me, but I would rather destroy it all then let Cat-7 keep it.

"Deploy Shai-Hulud, let me know when he's entrenched."

Deploying. Ten seconds for network saturation.

"Have they disconnected the communications net yet?"

Negative. Our intrusion is localized only but it will not remain so for long. Once they know we're here they will send reinforcements. I have confirmation of Shai-Hulud's spread to the next hub.

Excellent. The worm will work its way through Cat-7 and the longer they go without detecting it the more information I'll have. When I tapped into their corporate network I did something similar. But this isn't their official network, this is something else entirely.

"What the hell are they working on here?"

I believe this is the origination of the plasma gun technology and the quantum teleporter.

"Figures. Okay, time to go. Fire the EMP!"

I brace myself, I haven't exactly tested this yet. Theoretically, the suits shielding will hold. We came up with the idea after we fought the Creature. I doubled the shielding in the MKII for this very reason. One thumbnail sized ZPFM ejects from a compartment in my shoulders and explodes. The heat energy is minimal but the EMP is powerful and instant. My HUD dims as the pulse bursts every circuit, battery, hard drive and wipes any information kept on a magnetic or electronic media. The lights shatter and we're cast into darkness.

My HUD refreshes with an overlay of green night vision as well as thermographic. I can see heat sources hotter than ambient air which means people stick out like a sore thumb. I hadn't counted on them being unwilling participants in their own rescue. Think, Amelia, think!

Multiple quantum teleportation signals are blooming around the base.

"Reinforcements?"

I don't think so...

Several rapid pops and half the scientists in the room are gone. Oh no. Evacuation.

"Open comms to Kate, now Epic!"

I run over and scoop my parents up in my arms.

"Amelia?" Kate's groggy voice sounds in my ear.

"Kate, I need you right frigging now!"

Kate Petrenelli is my best friend for a reason. Before the sound is even done echoing in my helmet, she's here. Dressed in a modest pink nightie and slippers, she appears next to me.

"Arsenal, what the hell is going—"

"My parents, Domino, these are my parents. No time to explain, port them to my lab!"

Her eyes narrow but she doesn't say anything else. She touches my mom and the two of them vanish.

"Epic, as soon as we're back, full spectrum jamming on the lab. There's got to be a way to block the signal they're using to lock onto them."

Affirmative.

She's back with a pop, leaning over she takes my father and vanishes.

I watch as the last of the people in the room disappear like Kate. Is that how she does it? Is her teleportation quantum-based? I briefly wonder if they came up with their advanced tech by studying supers. They certainly have the access.

With a pop of displaced air, Kate is back. She puts her hands on my shoulders and—

We're in my lab.

"Full spectrum ECM now!"

Engaged.

"Okay Amelia," Kate says standing next to me in her nightie with sweat beading on her brow from the rapid teleports, "You want to tell me what the hell is going on?" Kate asks. Hands balled into fists on her hips and she looks none too happy.

It turns out Cat-7 uses a subdermal tracking implant to keep tabs on its people. Once the ECM was on they couldn't lock onto the implant. It survived the EMP because it's a radioactive marker, low-level enough it wouldn't harm my parents, but strong enough that Cat-7's sensors could pick up on it. Once the full jamming suite activated in my lab Mom and Dad were safe. The first thing we did was neutralize the tracker with a proton beam.

Currently, Mom and Dad are sleeping in an empathy-induced rest while I explain to Kate what's happened.

She isn't happy with me.

Wheeling around to my display I punch in a few more metrics. I thought maybe it wasn't them, that my memory was fooling me, but everything Epic has says they are indeed my parents.

"I don't understand why they don't remember me..." I say for the umpteenth time.

Kate has the far away look in her eyes she gets when reading people.

"You should have told us, Amelia, we could have helped," she says, blowing a strand of perfect black hair out of her eyes.

"I'm sorry. The more people knew the more likely Cat-7 would know I was on to them. It's taken me forever to find them, Kate, I just couldn't risk it," I tell her. Of course I'm not looking at her, I punch a couple more buttons and—

My chair jerks around and she's eye-level with me.

"We're friends, Amelia, or supposed to be. You should have trusted *me*." The pain in her voice is heartbreaking.

I am the dumbest smart person I know. I drop my face covering it with my hands. I was so wrapped up, so *focused* on my parents I hadn't even thought about telling her. What's worse, that I didn't trust her or I didn't *think* to even tell her? A hundred different words come to mind but all I do is sit there with my mouth open like an idiot. The genuine hurt on her face is killing me. What would Luke think when he found out? Would... would he break up with me? If he felt as betrayed as Kate does...

"Stop," she puts a gentle hand on the top of my head, "Self-pity tastes awful on you. And no, I doubt Luke will be as upset as me," she says cocking her head to one side to peer at me. "You really didn't think to include me did you?"

Having an empath for a friend, a best friend, has its ups and downs. Sometimes I feel like my conversations with her are me *feeling* things and her replying to them as if I had spoken. Regardless, her touch tells me she's passed it.

"I'm sorry Kate, I... I was so wrapped up in finding them, in knowing where they were, I fell into old habits. *Of course* I can trust you... do trust you. I just—I've been alone for a long time and when it all came down, I went back to instinct. I'm sorry." I'm terrible at this, I know. Since I was six years old the whole world has thought I was delusional. I had to stop talking about my parents or they would put me in counseling to 'actualize my grief'. I learned that lesson the hard way. I guess I need to 'unlearn' it.

She squats down to look me in the eye, raising my head with her fingers on my chin.

"You're not alone, Amelia, not anymore. Okay? We all believe you."

I can feel the tears welling and my heart is pounding as her face fills with warmth and a smile that makes it all better.

"It's okay," she says.

I smile back wiping my eyes for a second before I speak. "Why don't they know who I am?"

She gives me one more reassuring look before standing up and turning to evaluate my parents. Her eyes take on the distant look, a kind of unfocused gaze, as she uses her powers.

"Mind if I touch them?"

Her abilities work on many different levels, touch is one of them.

"Please do," I tell her. I look up at the big screen. Epic has the news from Boston on it. He's monitoring the situation, making sure I'm not mentioned. I don't think any cameras caught sight of me, especially since we hacked all the CCTV within a block of the building. I came down just before dawn so even a night vision camera wouldn't have worked well. So far, they are going with 'building fire'. Why hide what really happened? Unless it was an illegal building and they don't want to draw attention to it.

"There's something not right here," Kate says over her shoulder. I wheel over to see.

She has a hand on each of them and her face crinkles up like she smelled something bad.

"It isn't like anything I've seen before. There are different levels of manipulation. The basic stuff, like what I do passively is pretty harmless." She doesn't open her eyes as she speaks, just cocks her head to the side as if she were working through a puzzle. "If I try real hard I can make a man more attracted to me then he normally would be, but I couldn't persuade him to do anything he didn't already want to do. The next level is active persuasion. That is where I shift people's emotions and feelings in the direction I want them to go. Third level is where the low-level mind control starts to come to play. While I can do one and two better than just about anyone, mind control is strictly the domain of the telepath. And there just aren't a lot of them capable of this fine control. As far as I can tell, your parents are perfectly normal. If it wasn't for the fact that I've been reading people's emotions since I was fourteen I wouldn't even think there was anything wrong..."

"But you do think there is?" I say hopefully.

"Yes, there's something wrong, but it's slippery. I can't quite get a grasp on it."

I shake my head, if she can't fix it, what do I do? I'm no neurologist. In all my plans and backup plans, undoing brainwashing wasn't one of them. Stupid, really. Why didn't I think of this? Between my parents they have three advanced degrees. If they could have found a way to contact me they would have. I'd always assumed I'd been under some kind of threat and that was why but... now it all makes sense.

"Which begs the question, who could do this?" I ask Kate.

"I don't follow?"

"Every person with superpowers is on a list of some kind. Either through government registration or as a criminal, right? You said yourself, there aren't a lot of empaths and even fewer true telepaths, right?"

She nods, "Yeah. We went to a special school in New York state, up north away from people. Some of us were too dangerous to allow out and others, like myself, needed time to learn how to control our powers before we were safe around people. I think there was," she looks away for a second, "Fifteen or so students when I was there ten years ago. As far as I know, the rate of emergence of mind powers stays a fairly small percentage. The vast majority of supers get the F1 package, you know, better than normal vision, levitate a foot off the ground, that sort of the thing. The number one power set for F3's is speed, strength, and reflexes. The higher the rating the less often the powers emerge. I'm an F4 empath which is rare in itself, but only a small percentage of F5's are telepaths."

I nod, my mind whirling. If there is a school, then there is a list.

"Epic—"

Way ahead of you. Checking.

"If someone did mess with your parents' minds, and I am pretty sure they did, do you think they would have gone to the School? Mind control, true mind control, is dealt with pretty harshly. Our headmaster was the strongest telepath around and if he found out you were consciously using your abilities to force people to do things they didn't want to do..." she shivered. I don't think I've ever seen her afraid or upset before. This guy must be a piece of work.

Was his name Mr. Kana?

"That's the guy. When people think of mind control they think of big-brained individuals. Mr. Kana is from Samoa, the biggest man, and I am including

Luke when he's hulked out, I have ever seen. Six-seven if he was an inch and—"

Deceased.

Kate stumbles, her face flashing pale, "Dead? No, he was only ten years older than me... what happened?" She releases my parents and walks over to the screen where Epic displays the information. The screen fills with news stories of a mugging gone wrong and Mr. Kana tried and failed to intervene. He caught a bullet in the back of his head.

She shook her head, "No. Amelia, just... *no.*"

I look at her then my parents and back at her. I need her help to fix them but she is as distraught as I've ever seen her.

"What do you mean, 'no'?"

"You have to understand," she says, "He is... *was* an F5 Telepath, do you know what that means?"

F5's are the most dangerous of all powered people. They're rated based on how much property damage, or lives they can take in a given minute. They stop counting at F5. Once they got to the part where they could wipe out a city in a minute, giving them ratings above that just didn't make sense.

I shake my head, "I mean I know what an F5 is and I can only assume an F5 telepath is probably a big deal—"

She interrupts with a wave of her hand. "Not a big deal, *the big deal*. He worked with us because he loved kids and he wanted to see the people afflicted with the *curse* of empathy and telepathy make it. Do you know what the suicide rate for empaths and telepaths are?"

I shrug.

"If we're not found within a day of our abilities manifesting it is near eighty percent. No one makes it past a week without help. There's no blocking it out, no stopping it. You drown in other people's thoughts and emotions. They become yours. The only difference is, you have a hundred people inflicting their emotions on you all at once and you feel them all as if they were your own..."

She turns away, her shoulders hunching. She'd hinted at the difficulty she'd faced when her powers emerged, but I hadn't known, not really. Having no powers it feels uncomfortable trying to comfort her. How am I supposed to understand?

"You're not," she says with a sigh, letting out a long breath she shakes herself and stands tall. "You can't, not really. He could, though, Mr. Kana. This is why he wasn't killed by a mugger or in some stupid crime. With a thought, he could order any person alive to kill themselves. No, he was murdered. The question is, why?"

"I don't know why, but the who... I would guess it's the same people behind Cat-7. Epic, is the school still in operation?"

Yes.

"That's something. In the meantime, what do I do about my parents? I can't leave them in a coma and if they wake up they're just going to run back to Cat-7. This isn't how I imagined this going," I tell her. Frustration churns inside of me and I want to hit something, scream, or cry... possibly all three.

"I'm sorry Amelia, really," she says with a hand on my shoulder.

"Me too," I sigh.

"There's a private hospital in Seattle, for victims of telepaths and empaths. I could make a call, maybe get them admitted. I don't know if they can do anything for them, but it might help."

My heart leaps to seize just a little bit of hope.

"Let's do it."

Mind control. The database is pretty limited. In the last hundred years only a few dozen *true* telepaths emerged. Almost all of them F5's. Most rely on sound. Their voices trigger something in a person's mind forcing them, or persuading them, to do what the controller wants. A few can lock onto a person's brain waves and alter them or read them.

Ultimately, everything in our bodies is nothing more than a series of electrical impulses. If a power allows the manipulation of those impulses then it stands to reason said power must be able to *read* those impulses. This is all theoretical, but it is all I have. My lab is protected by a Faraday cage, this prevents any electronic spying or unwanted signals from escaping or entering my lab. *Theoretically,* it would also prevent any electromagnetic signal, including telepathy, to enter or exit.

Which is why I'm spraying a clear coat of metallic ink on my suit. The effect will make it slightly glittery in the sun, which isn't a bad thing, and it will add a Faraday cage to my external armor when powered. By itself it wouldn't be one-hundred percent effective. However, with the ZPFM powering it and the rest of my ECM suite I should be damn near invulnerable to mind control. The good thing is, my faceplate isn't really transparent I use micro-optic cables to simulate transparency. Which means my suit is fully coated in my new ink—

"Hey, you didn't show up for dinner." Luke's voice startles the crap out of me and I end up spraying the wall next to the helmet.

Dinner? At two in the afternoon?

I glance up at the TV and the timer in the bottom corner shows I'm off by about four hours.

"Luke, I'm so sorry I—"

He holds up his hand, "No, don't. Amelia. Would you get mad at me if I lost track of time at the gym?"

I shake my head, of course I wouldn't. Especially with the way his muscles ripple. Even now, when he's just wearing jeans, a white v-neck t-shirt and his cowboy hat... Luke has always done funny things to my insides. The way his smile touches his eyes when he sees me for the first time each day... that's the best part of all.

"So I won't get upset with you for mad-sciencing your armor and forgetting our date. Instead," he brings his hand out from behind him, "I shall bring dinner to you! Wallah!"

Pizza from Bianco's, oh how I love this man. I didn't mean that. Or did I? One more thing to think about.

Thirty minutes and three slices later we're on the couch watching Star Trek and cuddling. Possibly my favorite thing to do in the entire world. Cuddling, not Trek. Well, okay both.

Sadly, I can't quite focus on it. Kate suggested holding off telling anyone about my parents, for now. With a telepath on the loose as strong as it would take to kill her mentor, she's worried just having the knowledge would endanger them. I can't say she's wrong. Still, after the fact, it feels like lying. Something I have always hated to do, even when necessary.

"Amelia, what's wrong?"

"Are you sure you're not the empath?"

He chuckles. "It doesn't take an empath to tell your upset. Is it me? Am I presuming too much by staying here to the wee hours every night?"

Him? Oh no, he thinks I'm upset with him? Fix it, Amelia!

"No, not at all, I love having you here. Who else would fetch sodas for me at two in the morning? It's not that at all Luke," I say, resting my head against his chest.

"Is it Studio 50? I can always tell them you can't come."

Crap, I completely forgot about that. I need to work out some kind of calendar for Epic. Then again, he probably didn't remind me because he knows how much I don't want to go.

"No, I was thinking about my parents. How they... if they... if they were out there but for some reason couldn't remember me or didn't know me? Why else would they not find a way to let me know they're okay. I mean, I built Arsenal to find them and they're at least as smart as me, right? Between the two of them, they could have found a way."

He nods, "I'm sure they would, Amelia." He runs his hand through my hair and for a second I let it all go. Were they mind-controlled from the moment the accident happened? That would explain a lot.

I hate thinking about that day. On the flip side, I've thought of little else since the accident. The phone call. Mom called the accident in on the phone. I close my eyes and try to think back.

She handed the phone to dad. They both spoke on it. Then... I don't remember. Well, either they use voice control or brainwave control and I'm pretty sure I can defend against both. All the other feelings associated with that day leave me shivering. I've thought about it so many times it seems like it should get easier. It doesn't. Luke pulls me tight, bringing the blanket covering my legs up to my chin.

"Better?"

"Yes, yes I am, thanks."

"How much better?" he asks with a hungry look in his eyes.

"Why don't you kiss me and find out?"

The last time I was at the airport, the Psychotic Six tried to blow it up. This time is a little different. Apparently, as a registered superhero and with her powers properly identified, my Kate, with the BA in Marketing from Ohio State, can stand before a judge in her *mask* and testify to the condition of my parents. When asked how they came to be found, Kate towed the line between truth and lie.

"A concerned citizen turned them over to us."

Us, being the Arizona State Militia. Aka The Diamondbacks. She also told the judge, based on the level of manipulation, it would be best to keep their identities sealed, lest the controller find them. The problem with evil mind control powers is the complete lack of an ability to stop them. Except for me of course.

"I'm still not sure what we're doing here, we should be at work. Why are we in Arizona and not Boston?" I hear my dad say. My heart cracks open and I want to scream. Instead, all I can do is stand here and play guard dog. It was the only way I was going to see them again.

Kate has her hand on each of their shoulders in a move I know well. She's using maximum effort to influence them. Unlike a telepath, who can outright force people to do things, Kate uses her God-given charm, knowledge of psychology, pheromones, and empathic touch in a combination few can resist.

"Mr. Lockheart, I explained this. A telepath has altered your memories, altered your perceptions. I'm one of the good guys here. We're taking you and your wife to a safe place where you can heal. It's important you try to remember who you are. Focus on your love for each other and I promise you will find your way through this."

He nods, his hand is in Mom's and they glance at each other with a soft smile I remember them sharing often. More than anything I want to climb out of this armor and hug both of them. My fist clenches and I try real hard to stay calm. It isn't working.

I've never wanted to murder anyone in my life, but if I find the person responsible for this...

"Arsenal, they're leaving," Kate interrupts my felonious thoughts.

I want to say something. Try to explain who I am again. Kate says there is no getting through to them; the memories are locked up tight behind a wall of their own creation.

"Have a good flight," I say instead.

I watch as they walk through the terminal, hand-in-hand. I watch as they take one last look behind before exiting the building to board the private gulf stream I arranged. The plane takes off without incident and I track it as far as the airport's radar goes. Then I stand there some more. I don't want to go. I found them. I *found* them. And they are gone again. It isn't fair.

Someone is going to pay.

"Epic, status on Shai-Hulud?"

He has successfully infiltrated their network. However, he is limited in communications. Their security is incredibly sophisticated. He can send one-kilobyte of data every twenty-four hours.

"What happens if we go for broke and have him send what he can before they shut down the system?"

There is no way of calculating the odds of retrieving useful information.

"Penny for your thoughts, the non-murderous ones?" Kate asks. Crap, I've been standing here for twenty minutes staring north and she has stood silently next to me the whole time.

"I want whoever did this, Domino. I want them dead," I hold up my hand to forestall her, "and if I can't have them dead, then I will see them rot in prison for the rest of their stinking life."

She nods, "I believe you... the question is, what's next?"

Mom and Dad are safe, at least. Maybe even on their way to a cure. That leaves two avenues. Kate's old mentor, Mr. Kana, and Shai-Hulud.

"I'm gonna fly, clear my head. I'll meet you back at HQ and we'll go from there."

She cocks her head sideways at me and I know what she's thinking.

"Honest, no taking off on my own. I need you."

"Okay. You know I'm here for you." She places her hand on my shoulder and smiles. The air pops and she's gone.

I walk out of the airport and blast off. I'm a few thousand feet up and I let Epic take the wheel so I can think. He puts me into an orbit over Phoenix. As I see it I have a few problems.

Who took my parents?

Why?

I have to assume that Category-7, the Cabal, and whoever let the Psychotic Six out of prison, are all the same people. The real question then is, what are they after? They had my parents slaving away for fourteen years building tech. From what I saw, my parents and a lot of other scientists. Did they kidnap them all? For a while I thought they wanted my armor, and maybe they did or do. Are they amassing a hi-tech arsenal?

"Epic, run a search: missing scientists and cross-reference it with telepaths."

Time parameter?

Good question... "Twenty-years."

Affirmative.

Missing scientists, dead telepaths, and hi-tech weapons along with several attempts to steal my armor. Whoever is behind it is hoarding technology, scientists, and possibly killing of telepaths?

Why?

Search complete. In the last twenty years, fifteen scientists, including your parents, have disappeared without a trace. One day they existed, then they didn't.

If it wasn't for the Internet I wouldn't have even known about them. In that same time frame, three F4, and one F5 telepath have died or disappeared under suspicious circumstances.

"It would be safe to assume then, whoever's behind this can mind control. Maybe that is the reason for killing the other telepaths?"

You have an incoming call from Luke.

"On screen," I say with a smile. Whatever dour thoughts I have vanish when I see his smiling mug.

"Amelia, where are you?"

"Flying over Phoenix, doing some thinking. Is there an alert?"

"No, but Pierre, Tommy and I have to go. The Governor is off to DC for a special summit with the head of the DMHA. She wants us there to show the flag. I'm leaving Kate in charge, so try not to get in trouble while we're gone?"

"No promises." I can hear him sigh. "How long are you going to be gone?"

"Just a couple of days. Hey, aren't you supposed to be in LA at five?"

Crap! Yes I am.

"I've got plenty of time," I say convincingly.

You don't, actually. We will have to exceed Mach Three to make it there before your scheduled interview.

"Okay then, have fun. Don't blow a hole in the studio or anything, and I'll see you when I get back. And Amelia?"

I smile at the thought of going nuclear on the stupid show, "Yes?"

"I... I'll miss you."

11

"**W**e're here today with the *hero* of Las Vegas, Arsenal," the show's host says. I already dislike this woman. The way she emphasized hero didn't sound like a compliment. Luckily, no one can see my face. While I have to do this show as part of my 'duties' to the team, I don't have to do it out of the armor. Instead, I'm on their couch in three-hundred pounds of titanium and tungsten. I've never really paid much attention to this person or the show itself. I had to have Epic give me the lowdown.

Ranna 'Make it Rain' Meadows was a superhero with the invaluable power of making it rain in a localized area. Epic says she did a stint on the SoCal team, which according to Luke pretty much anyone can get on, powers or no. I imagine she could be handy in a forest fire, but not a lot else.

She's pretty, not Kate, but pretty. California has a way of homogenizing people into tanned skin and blonde hair, and she certainly fits the bill. Her shows tend to be light, funny, and occasionally she has dramatic reveals. A few well-known supers have admitted to crimes on her shows and a couple of gone public with their identity here. I had Epic play me the tapes and I thought it was odd, after all, if I were going to admit to a crime it wouldn't be on national TV. Regardless, she has the highest rated talk show in the US for that very reason.

"Tell us about yourself, Arsenal?" she asks with a vapid expression. I can't really read her, it's like she's playing poker. The set would be intimidating if I weren't hiding in my armor. Numerous LED lights illuminate every square inch. They have three cameras they use to catch the guests at different angles. Epic offered to hack them to make sure they caught my best side.

"There's nothing really to tell. I've always dreamed of being a superhero," that's an easy lie, who doesn't? "When I didn't manifest with powers I found a way to simulate them. Hence the suit." I shrug. This is the cover lie Kate helped me come up with. Part lie, part truth. I've never dreamed of having super powers but that is for me to know.

"And what was it like, the first time you flew?"

I was expecting more of a focus on the incident in Vegas since that's the reason I'm even doing the interview, but whatever.

"Pretty cool. Flying is far and away the most awesome thing to do in the suit." I tell her.

Her eyes narrow and she cocks her head to the side a little. It's like she's trying to see through my faceplate or something. Her hand plays with her coffee cup as a few seconds go by. Maybe she's trying to read me? Fat chance. Not only can she not see my face, the suit obliterates body language not to mention Epic adjusts my voice to remove all traces of emotion.

"Hmm, laconic I see. How long have you been with the Diamondbacks—"

I open my mouth to answer but she keeps on going—

"And is it true you're romantically linked to Major Force?"

Anger flushes through me, freezing my thoughts as my whole body goes stiff. How could she possibly know that?

Careful, she is trying to manipulate you into divulging information. Let me process the—

"Thanks, Epic, I got this," I say to him. I take a breath to stifle my anger at her invasion and say, "Major Force is an exceptional team leader and a selfless human being. Any woman would be lucky to call him a boyfriend." Thank goodness Epic flattens my voice; I couldn't keep it from wavering. Of course it's none of her business. None. But she is in it for the money, she does this for the ratings and the juicier the better, right?

I can tell she's not happy with my answer. Again, she cocks her head to the side... what is she trying to do?

"Let's try another line, I see you've added glitter to your suit? Is that to remind the public you are a woman? You are a woman, aren't you? You're not a man hiding in that suit?"

Glitter? I didn't add glitter—my spray Faraday shield! There must be a lot of EMR in the room for it to sparkle like that. It's causing the electrons on the outside to flash, I guess that would look like glitter. I figured in the bright sun it would sparkle but this is something else.

"Epic, run a full diagnostics, make sure we're okay and bring the ECM suite to 'active'."

Affirmative.

"Well, I am a gir—woman, I do like shiny things," I mock laugh. I can only imagine how awkward an emotionless laugh must sound.

She takes a sip of her coffee while looking at me over the rim of the cup. Maybe I should take charge of this before I let her dictate the whole thing to me.

"When I was in Las Vegas I—"

"Tell me," she talks right over me, "If you're not romantically involved with Major Force, surely there must be someone who you're involved with? Perhaps Domino?"

My brain short circuits and I can't think of anything to say to that.

"Surely, with a team as tight as the Diamondbacks, someone is sleeping with someone. I know our audience would love to know."

"What the hell kind of question is that?" Does this line usually work for her? I can't imagine anything I would want to talk about less than my love life or anyone else's.

She blinks several times before sitting up straight. Her eyes narrow and I can't tell what she thinks she's trying to do. After a moment she gives herself a little shake and turns to the camera.

"We'll be right back after these commercials."

She holds a vapid smile for a second then the red light on the camera vanishes and she turns to me, all pretense of civility is gone and she practically snarls.

"What kind of robot are you? I was told there's a real person under all that armor? Paulsen? Paulsen?" she screams at the booth above the soundstage.

There's a click of an electronic microphone kicking in, "Yes, Ranna?" a man asks with equal parts resignation and boredom.

"Do we have a backup guest? What about the guy in the green tights? The one with the bird name?" she has gone from glowering to ignoring me. I would be offended if I knew what the hell was going on.

"No backup guests, this is a major spot for us, no one else has interviewed Arsenal other than her local paper. Make it work, Ranna."

"Make it work? She's a damn robot, Paulsen, how am I supposed to get anything out of her?"

There's no response but the woman behind the camera shouts, "thirty seconds."

She turns to me in a huff and puts her palms flat down on her desk, "Now listen up, you stupid machine, give me something I can get ratings on."

"First," I reply, "I'm not a frigging robot. Okay? I'm here to talk about Las Vegas or anything else related to the *team*. Not their love lives or anything personal about them. If you're not happy with that I can leave right now." I stand up to emphasize my point. Her eyes narrow to dots as she glares at me.

I don't really care. I came here because Cat-7 made me. I can leave just as easy.

"Sit down," she orders.

There is something off about her. Our Faraday cage glowing could be interference from the wireless broadcasts... or something else.

Now that I think about it, he could be right. Could she be hiding empathic powers? Regardless, it won't, or shouldn't, affect me. Hopefully, she's got her act together now...

12

An hour later I'm on the roof of the TV building staring up into the smog-filled sky. I can't smell the air but I imagine it stinks. The sun is just about to start going down, and like the sun, my mood is plummeting. I can't help but feel hollow about this. Stupid interview aside, I feel like I'm missing something obvious.

Artemis has achieved a geosynchronous orbit above the Midwestern united states. I estimate she will be online in the next 24 hours.

"Thanks, buddy, good to know. Any word from Shai-Hulud?"

So far, he has identified three bases the enemy has. He has also delivered information about their organization. From what I have pieced together, and based on our new information, I would be 88% certain that the majority of Cat-7's 'shadow' organization we are now calling, 'The Cabal', are mind controlled assets.

That's sobering.

"Who on Earth could be powerful enough to control so many people at once?"

No one alive.

"You mean Kate's old headmaster? You think he faked his death?"

She did indicate the unlikeliness of his murder.

I mull that over for a second. The roar of a jet taking off at the airport booms over us as I think.

"Call Kate and..."

We are being jammed.

Roar of a jet? We're nowhere near—too late.

The explosion sends me sprawling off the roof of the twenty story TV station. My HUD flashes red over a number of subsystems as I tumble. The g-forces pull against me, my stomach threatens revolt.

"Kinetic shields, kinetic shields," I scream.

The ground comes up fast, I close my eyes bracing for impact. My momentum halts suddenly as the shields come back online absorbing the energy of the fall. I hit the ground with no more force than a step.

"What hit us?"

Unknown. The force of the blast was several thousand pounds.

A shadow falls over me. A cloud? No, much, much worse. I've seen the footage but... *Colossal.*

Data suggest you are facing a group of mercs known as 'Death Dealers'. They sell their powers to the highest bidder.

Fantastic. I hit the jets full power as a giant foot, at least ten feet long slams into the ground behind me. Concrete shatters like glass, cars flip and alarms ring. I need altitude. The roar of a jet engine fills the air. It wasn't a plane before, but whatever knocked me off the roof. I dodge hard right as a fireball streaks by. The sensor suite in my optics darkens the glaring blaze showing the man inside.

"Besides Colossal and Rocketman, who else does the team have?" I turn and fire IP canons full power back the way I came. The energy smashes into Colossal, dissipating off the surface area of his skin.

He's easily sixty feet tall with a black and white spandex-like suit. It stretches and covers him head to toe. Thankfully, he isn't as fast as a normal sized person, but certainly tougher. He's between two buildings, using one as a support as he swats at me. The other guy, some kind of human rocket, keeps barreling down on me.

"Are there more than two?"

The details of their roster are sketchy at best. Colossal is the most well known for his rampage in Puerto Rico, there are likely three to four members total.

Awesome. I swerve just in time to avoid Rocketman, again. He can't bank worth a damn. However, with his body burning the way it is, I can't exactly pod him. I seriously doubt a pod will have any effect on Colossal either.

I burn straight up, flip over reversing my course effectively looping up above the big guy so he can't hit me as I fly behind him.

"Scan that parked fire truck, anyone in it?"

Two firefighters.

I land in front of the truck with a crunch of shattered concrete. The two firefighters in the cab stare at me open-mouthed. I thought people in LA would be used to seeing supers? Epic pumps up the volume on my voice.

"Get out!"

They don't hesitate.

"Three pods, front, middle, back."

I don't have a lot of time, Rocket is coming around for another strafing run and there may still be two other attackers hiding in the concrete canyons of downtown LA. As we climb I hear my grenade launcher sing its quire of *puff puff puff*.

Colossal turns around, managing to carve out enough of the buildings he's using for balance to create an avalanche of glass and steel. Damn. Where is the SoCal team? This should be all over the news?

"What's with the jamming? Any chance we can find the source?"

Scanning. They have a tight beam directional jammer tracking us. I will try to triangulate as you fly. Do not get hit.

"Gee, you think?"

Rocketman screams by. I spin to avoid him sending a stream of IP cannons after him but he's too fast for me to follow, the energy just ends up washing against the side of a building. At least in the narrow canyons he can't turn around with any speed.

"Any chance Artemis is ready?"

Negative, while she is in a stable orbit, she has yet to fully deploy her package.

A glance at the firetruck and she's still only a few feet off the ground. Just a few more seconds and she'll be high enough for my plan to work. Seconds I might not get. I bank again, coming around a tall circular building and I see a man standing on top of it. He has long black hair tied in a ponytail and one of those long beards I see everyone sporting suddenly. Dressed like a logger he holds his hand out at me with his fingers shaped like a gun.

"Epic—"

He pretend fires and the world explodes. Flames engulf the suit, master alarms scream, the sheer force blasts me through glass windows and drywall and out the other side. The concrete firewall of the first floor stops me cold. Screams of panic fill the air. As my vision clears I can see the hole we made, thirty feet long and smoking. The buildings fire alarm sounds and water sprays down instantly turning to steam on contact with the suit. If I had been in the MKI— I'd be dead now.

"Who the hell is that?" I ask. My legs are wobbly but they do the job.

Hand Cannon. He can project massive pyrotechnic explosions from his forefinger. Based on what hit us I would say an order of magnitude greater than any missile or bomb. While the kinetic shields can absorb the secondary effects, the initial blast hits the armor.

A glance at my chest and sure enough, a blackened scorch mark covers it dead center as if a bomb went off right in front of me. The suit is tough, but it's designed to work with the shields.

"Okay, they want to play rough, no more Ms. Nice Girl. Safeties off."

On the HUD the particle beam ready light flicks on. Both power up instantly.

Kinetic Lance is also at one-hundred percent.

Thankfully the office I hit was mostly empty; I don't think anyone was hurt. I trigger my Emdrive and floor it out the hole I made when I entered. Rocketman must have been waiting because he's on my tail in an instant. Epic fires the Lance as soon as I bracket his blazing form. He jerks up like he hit a wall and careens away in a spiral toward the ground.

I can't help but smile.

"Okay, status on the fire truck?"

Thirty feet up.

"Perfect."

Staying low to avoid Hand Cannon, I swing back around, dodge a chunk of wall Colossal throws at me and fly between his legs. The fire truck is only sixty feet away, it takes a little less than two seconds to cover that. I line up behind it and trigger the afterburners. The truck probably weighs five tons. Five tons that my ag pods manage to nullify. However, force isn't calculated using weight, it's calculated using mass.

I slam the truck into his back at a hundred miles an hour. The mass of the fire truck is a thousand times greater than I could achieve on my own and the impact crushes bones and pulps flesh. He goes down screaming. The forward pod is destroyed when the cab of the truck caves. I let it go to glide gently to the ground.

Colossal shrieks in pain all the way down. His powers cut off and by the time he's writing in agony the big man is nothing more than his usual height.

"Pod him," I tell Epic.

Puff.

Now, that just leaves—

Fire and noise rains down and I tumble a hundred feet to the ground slamming into concrete and digging a furrow twenty feet long. My HUD flashes an angry red at me as system after system reports failure.

Kinetic shielding 30%

Particle Beams—Offline

IP Cannons—Offline

Kinetic Lance—Offline

I manage to roll onto my back with a groan. All the things I've invented and this whack job with a stupid name is going to kill me. Real fear runs through my veins. Blood roars in my ears and my brain panics, scrambling for anything to reverse this.

Propulsion—Offline.

A shadow falls over me as I try to stand. Hand Cannon drops to the ground a dozen yards away.

"You're a tough piece of work, but at the end of the day— you're only human."

He lifts his hand, finger out.

"Epic..."

A shadow slices across the sky and a bronze-tipped spear slams into the ground between us. Confusion passes across his face and mine. A spear? He straightens his hand out and 'pulls the trigger'. Six feet of Spartan god slams the ground between us, shield facing Hand Cannon. The explosion impacts on the surface of the bronze shield. Fire and pressure shunt to the sides as if it hit a wall. Rocks and debris fill the air clouding my vision for a moment.

When the debris settles, Protector lowers his undamaged shield. He gestures toward the spear. The ancient looking weapon leaps from the ground and flies through the air to smack against his outstretched hand. I've only ever seen him one time in person, sitting in the cafeteria at the Portland base. On TV? A hundred times. He is the most well-known superhero in the world. He's also one of the few who doesn't operate on a team. After all, who could make him? He can go anywhere in the world, he's nigh-invulnerable, and is so strong his upper limit can't be measured as there is nothing heavy enough to test it. When I was sixteen he pulled a sinking *cruise ship* to shore using her anchor.

"It's over, Harold," he says in a deep voice, that resonates even through my armor while pointing his spear at Hand Cannon... Is his name Harold?

Systems rebooting... thirty seconds to full restoration, Epic informs me.

"You can't just come in here and save the day. You don't get to do that!" Harold raises his hand to fire again. Protector flashes forward faster than Fleet could and slams his round shield into Harold's chest sending him flying back twenty feet. Before he's hit the ground Protector is on him. With one punch Harold collapses.

Protector stands and looks around for a few seconds, his steely brown eyes scanning for threats.

Say thank you, Epic prompts on the screen.

"Right! Uh, thank you sir, Protector, sir." I stammer. It's one thing to see him on TV but... he's amazing!

"Arsenal, right?" He says in a much softer tone as he walks over to help me up.

"Yes, sir," I say. I don't know why I'm suddenly saying sir. It's just... he's the only superhero I ever really paid attention to. He always seemed so incorruptible, so full of hope.

"You can call me Syd, saying 'Protector' every few seconds is a mouthful," he says with a sly smile. His helmet covers his head but his eyes and mouth are perfectly clear.

He pulls me up no problem.

Jamming has died. Authorities are en route. I've notified the local DMHA officer along with the US Marshals Service. ETA thirty-seconds.

"Thank you, Syd, I was about to have my but whooped."

"About?" He says with a chuckle.

"Fine, my butt was whooped." My arms feel like rubber and if I didn't have to fly back to Phoenix I could sleep right now. I put my feet together to blast off when he puts his hand on my shoulder.

"I need to talk to you... somewhere else. Mind if I drive?"

Drive? I nod. I have no idea what he means but if there is anyone I can trust, it's the man who just saved my life.

Flashing red and blue lights arrive freeing us to leave. I have Epic upload the footage to the locals and the US Marshals, that way I don't have to stick around and answer a million questions. I give Protector—I mean Sydney – the thumbs. I'm ready to go.

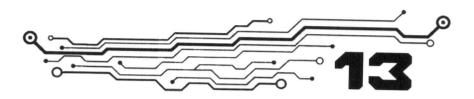

13

Sydney... such a normal name for a not normal person. It sounds weird calling him that instead of Protector.

He reaches around my waist and says, "Hold on." With his free hand, he reaches back and hurls the spear into the sky. I'm not sure what—

Holy crap! Air rushes by in a roar. Epic doesn't even have time to tell me how fast we're moving. I blink and we're in orbit.

Orbit!

Earth, from here is a big, beautiful blue and green gem spinning majestically below us.

I think the DMHA database is woefully misinformed about his powers. He does not teleport, but he certainly does not fly either.

I want to say something but my mouth just hangs open. Ever since our fight with the Six I've wanted to do this and here we are, in orbit. Sensors pick up the vacuum around us, a slight radioactive emanation from the Van Allen belt, and lots and lots of space. Lots. He keeps a firm grip on me otherwise I would be turning to see the moon and beyond.

We're holding relatively still as the Earth rotates below us. I've seen the ISS camera as it traverses the Earth several times a day but seeing how fast the planet spins when were stationary is breathtaking. The East coast goes by, then the Atlantic ocean, Spain, then Italy—

He hurls his spear down, it vanishes in a second, leaving only a red trail from friction as it passes through the atmosphere. The next second we're right behind it. Air roaring by in a heartbeat and then we hit the ground. I stumble a few feet with my hands out, my inner ear insisting that we're still moving.

"Holy crap!"

"I'm sorry, I forget how disorienting and frightening that—"

"Are you kidding me? That was frigging awesome!" I shout.

We are in Greece, Delphi to be exact.

"I'm glad you like it. After all these years of doing it, I still get a rush. Come, this way." He marches forward to the old ruins. I've never really studied history, not the way I do physics and math. I've read a few, mostly American history. I have to admit, I'm partial to history around inventors like Ben Franklin and scientists like Newton.

However, this temple seems familiar, I think I've seen it in a movie or TV show. Crumbling rocks and broken down arches dot the area. What little grass there is has a nice green color. In the distance, I see a modern city with the haze of pollution obscuring the skyline. If it weren't for that I could almost believe we were back in time.

GPS location confirmed. This is the Oracle at Delphi. An archaeological site where in ancient times the Greek people would come to consult Pythia, a high priestess of Apollo. A woman gifted with incredible powers of prophecy, or so myth tells us. The site was last used for this purpose in roughly the fourth century AD.

"Is this where you hang your helmet when you're not saving armored damsels in distress?"

"Something like that."

Following him is like following a wall of muscle and steel. He's huge and when he walks I can see the ripples beneath his skin. His breastplate, leather skirt, and sandals all look like he stepped out of an old movie. He leads me around the back of the ancient ruins that are little more than standing stones and crumbling foundations.

He turns and smiles while he reaches for a pillar. His fingers brush a hidden button and there is an audible click.

"Stand here," he points to the ground next to him. "There are things about me others don't know. They can never know," he says while taking his helmet off. His eyes are the darkest brown I have ever seen. He steps closer to me and I fight the urge to step away. "But I'm told you're trustworthy."

"I like to think I am," I say lamely. How to accept a compliment like that graciously is beyond me.

The ground shakes for a moment then *lowers*. It's an elevator! We pass through the level of dirt and stone and a door slides shut above us once below ground level. From beneath a blue light emanates lighting up a cavern in a soft light. The underground cave is amazing, a languid waterfall splashes into a small pond in one corner. Light beams into the room from behind the water giving which is where the blue light comes from. I've never seen water so blue.

It is a good thing you moved me into the armor. This room is one-hundred percent signal proof. I would like to inquire as to how they have achieved that.

When the platform halts Sydney steps off toward the far corner where a mannequin stands. He places his helmet on it, then leans his shield down. When he unbuckles his chest piece my palms start to sweat. I know he saved me and all but I hope he didn't get the wrong idea...

"How did you know this place existed?" I ask, trying to divert my nervousness. "This has to be one of the most explored historical sites in the world. I'm stunned no one's discovered this underground chamber."

"It's on a separate plane of existence from ours. Parallel to Earth, but off by a hairsbreadth. Or, at least that is how it was explained to me." He finishes pulling the breastplate off, leaving him dressed in a simple knee-length red tunic, not unlike the ones the Spartans and Romans wore. All respect to Luke, but damn this man has muscles on his muscles.

"You're saying we aren't on Earth anymore?" My nerves vanish with the scientific implication of his words.

He nods, "I don't understand all of the details, but Pythia does and she is the one who told me to bring you here. While the powers I wield are great," he turns and waves his hand around the room, "they're only half the equation."

"Did you say Pythia?"

"That would be me," a little girl's voice says from behind. I leap in shock, stumbling forward and scrambling for footing as I turn to face an olive-skinned girl with long braided black hair and impossibly large eyes. She can't be older than thirteen, dressed in sleeveless white robes with intricate gold stitching running on either side down to the floor. She smiles patiently with her hands clasped in front of her while I recover.

I can see and hear her, but Amelia, she is not there in any other respect. No vitals, no thermal variances, nothing.

"Are you saying she's an apparition?" I ask Epic.

She laughs, "No, tell your computer I am no apparition."

Now both Epic and I are speechless. My armor is sound proof. Epic does a fantastic job of knowing when I'm talking to him or the people around me... she couldn't have heard me let alone know Epic is a computer.

"What... what are you?" I ask.

"I am Pythia, High Priestess of Apollo, Oracle of Time and Guardian of the Gates of Olympus."

"Right."

She smiles, "It amazes me, Amelia, that you invented a machine to walk for you, fly for you, think for you, yet are these the only impossible things allowed?"

Stun round number two... how the hell does she know who I am?

She gestures toward the far wall. The light level raises revealing a large wooden table with a spread of food that would make a king envious. Fruit, meat, cheese, drink, the whole nine yards. Protector claps his hands and practically runs over, "I'm starving," he says straddling the bench seats and digging in.

When Wardenclyffe Tower went online in 1903, Nikola Tesla and three square miles of New York vanished in an explosion that blew out windows in Manhattan. The best scientist of the day couldn't figure out what happened to him. Von Braun, the German scientist who eventually joined America after World War Two was the one who broke the forty-five-year-old mystery. Tesla had opened holes into other dimensions. Superpowers were nothing more than the physics or reality of another dimension inhabiting one person. Who, how, and why we're still, and are still a mystery.

I guess if I accept that, then I must accept this... to a point. I don't for one second think the gods of Olympus are real. However, Mr. Perfect thinks his magic is real, and regardless of what I believe, he does have a flying carpet.

"Give me a second, I usually catch on pretty quick but this is a bit much. You want to tell me how you know who I am?"

"Please, join us?" she says moving to the table. A plate of food, with all of my favorites including a cold can of open Coke with a straw sticking out, sits across from Sydney. He's busy wolfing down sliced ham, cheese, and the occasional grape.

"No strawberries huh?" I say as I walk around the table. Sitting in the armor is never easy. While it is flexible, it is only flexible to a point. I can't cross my legs or do fifty other things non-armored people can. I slip as best I can into the bench like seating. Epic triggers my faceplate so I can try the food if I want. I eye that straw, the conundrum of this is firing around my brain like a Gatling gun.

"You're very interesting Amelia. By far and away you are the most clever mortal we've ever met."

"Well, you are like five minutes younger than me so how many could you have met?"

She laughs and it's like chimes and bells.

"She's a lot older than she looks," Sydney says between bites. "I know this is hard for you to accept, I've read enough sci-fi to know the science-minded find it difficult to imagine things they can't prove, but trust me, she's the real deal," Sydney says with an earnest expression.

I nod, "How can you be sure she's just not a figment of your powers?"

He takes a long drink from a bronze cup, "Good question. Mostly, because I don't have any powers."

I laugh, he's pulling my leg... He's not pulling my leg.

"You're The Protector... I watched you pull a cruise ship... A *cruise ship* to shore using the anchor.

And then just today you stood up to Hand Cannon with your shield and..."

Oh. That's not possible... my mind scrambles for another explanation.

Pythias eyes light up and she giggles, "She is clever! I believe you mortals call it Ochams Razor."

"All things being equal, the simplest explanation is most often the true one... Your armor? Your powers come from the armor?"

I suddenly wish very much I had his shield in my lab.

"All of them, in a way. Putting the armor on infuses me with the strength of Hercules, the speed of Mercury, etc. But the real power is the Armor. If I were ever killed, Pythia would simply find some other worthy wielder."

How? His armor is bronze, it looks awesome, right out of Spartacus, but all the same, it's bronze.

"Let's pretend I believe this. There are supers who have armor besides me, though none of their armor operates without them. They're all elementals or mentally controlling constructs they wear. You're saying the bronze shield leaning against the mannequin is really *Aegis?* Like from the movie?"

He smiles, "Now you're getting it. Aegis is the shield, the breastplate belonged to Hercules, the spear was forged by Hephaestus for Achilles. The helmet was a gift to Leonidas from Athena. She granted him his wish to defend Sparta from the Persians."

I shake my head, "Okay, okay, I get it. Ancient Greek gods and artifacts of power. Wow. Okay." I raise my hands, "I know when I'm beat," I grin, "Now tell me why you are sharing all this with me? The person least likely to believe any of it?"

Sydney pushes his plate aside, "Do you want to tell her or should I?"

Pythia glides over and straddles the bench beside me, looking up at me with her eyes like dark pools.

"Amelia, of all the heroes you were drawn to Sydney as a child, why?"

I open my mouth to speak when I clamp it shut. She couldn't possibly know that... the wiggle of her eyebrow tells me she knows exactly what I was thinking. Either my telepathic defenses on the armor aren't working, which I doubt is true, or there are some things I'm going to have to accept on faith... for now. I glance at the straw. That I like Coca-Cola would be easy enough to divine. Heck, most of this she could know through hacking or careful observation. But there is no way, at least no way I can imagine other than what she is telling me, she could know I needed a straw to drink while I'm wearing the armor. Just no way. I decide to proceed as if what they say is the truth. For now.

"Hope," I say. "He gave me hope."

She nods, "Exactly as he's supposed to. When the gods lived on Earth, before the natural dimensional orbit drifted from their home plane, they tortured humanity with petty wars and affairs. Since then they have... matured. The guilt they feel over how they treated humanity eats at them. When Nikola Tesla turned on his machine they were given a chance to right a great wrong. Sydney and I... we work together to help humanity."

"This is all very interesting, but how do I fit in?"

"She's the Oracle, Amelia, she sends me on my missions. With the spear, I can be anywhere in the world a few seconds. How do you think I know where to go? Why do you think I knew exactly when to show up today to save you?"

Okay. I'm trying real hard to accept what they're saying. Otherwise, The Protector, the most powerful human being on the planet, is out of his mind crazy. I really could go either way at the moment. However, there is an abundance of proof he's not.

"Sydney gives humanity something to hope for and with my powers, I try to guide him to do the most good. As he said, I'm an oracle. However, I can't see the future, per se, but I can see probabilities. Likely outcomes of actions. I am... somewhat omniscient. I see thousands of futures, sometimes of an individual, like you, and sometimes of all of humanity."

I put a grape in my mouth, they're delicious and I try to keep my skepticism in check. "You can see the future? Okay, cool. Again though, why bring me here?"

Sydney glances over at Pythia, I can tell there is something even more pressing they want to share, but are concerned about how I'll react.

"Listen. You two obviously want to say something, and trust me, anything you have to tell me is going to be easier to accept than ancient Greek gods seeing the future and gifting humanity with a champion. I love sci-fi, not fantasy, this is all much harder to accept then you know. But as long as we're shooting for the moon here, let's pull all our cards on the table."

Pythia nods, her smile lights her eyes and she speaks, "Amelia, humanity is in great danger. Fifteen years ago we had an infinite amount of futures. A year ago we had thousands. Six months ago, a few hundred."

A lump forms in my throat, I don't like where this is going. "And now?"

"Two," she says quietly.

"I take it these two options aren't awesome?"

She shakes her head. "Something terrible is coming. There is nothing that can stop it. Sydney and I have tried. Whatever is coming can... *hide* from us, I don't know how. No action we take makes a difference for long. We've delayed for as long as we can and honestly I don't know if we've made it worse or better." She sighs with a shake of her head. Whatever else she might be, she genuinely cares I can see it in her eyes. "Three months ago things changed. I don't know exactly how, but your team had just defeated The Creature when it happened. We went from one horrible future to two. At first, I thought this was good... but it isn't, Amelia. Whatever force is driving humanity forward, it's driving them toward slavery and despotism. A tyranny unlike the world has ever seen."

I... I knew something bad was out there. Whoever took my parents, the people behind the weapons and the robots, the mind control... they had to have a plan and the only plan that made sense was this. Her words make more than one thing click into place. They want to conquer the world. As crazy as it sounds, it makes sense. A sufficiently powerful telepath could do it. Hitler was the last person to try and even he knew he couldn't have it all. No Army could ever keep the whole world in check, but a telepath? Yeah, they could... maybe. It would have to be one crazy powerful telepath, though.

"I don't know how they're hiding from you, but they can't hide from me. They took my parents, Pythia, they took my life. And now you're telling me they will take even more from everyone I care about? No worries, you may not be able to stop them, but I can." This is exactly what I needed. Independent confirmation. Her crazy aside, she obviously knows the whole story which means I'm on the right track.

"No, Amelia." her voice pulls my soul and I can see the sorrow in her eyes as she speaks. "Despotism is the best outcome. The other, the one where you continue your crusade, it ends with the death of humanity. The extinction of your people from the face of the Earth. For the good of the future, Amelia Lockheart, you must stop. Let events take their natural course. In a few centuries, the natural ebb and flow of humanity will correct the wrong and overthrow the shackles of tyranny. However, this is the *only* future humanity has. You must let it play out. If you don't stop, if you don't let it go, then humanity has no future, because there won't be any humans left."

A famous religious passage says there is nothing new under the sun. I respectfully disagree.

-Notes On an Electronic Life, by Epic

The screen shakes as GAME OVER scrolls across. My avatar lies dead and Carlos chuckles as he pops another Coke.

"Someone's on fire," he says before swallowing half the can in a few seconds.

I try to care, but Pythia's words have haunted me since I returned. All of this, laid in a grave and I'm the one who's going to cause it? I don't know how to be okay with ending humanity? Do I believe she is the Oracle of Delphi? The prophetess of Apollo? No. But, results speak for themselves. Whatever power she has is real, regardless of where it comes from. The evidence is too great to deny it.

"Amelia? Hello?" Carlos waves his hands in front of my face. He's crouched down looking up at me with his puppy dog eyes.

"You've been staring off into space for a good minute, everything okay?"

"Sorry... sorry," I run a hand through my hair, "Hero stuff on my mind."

"I can tell; I don't think I've ever beat you three times in a row. What's going on?"

I want to tell him about my parents about everything. How do I say, "An immortal oracle of an ancient god told me if I don't stop going after the man who stole my parents I'm going to destroy the world..."

I shake my head. I can't tell anyone except Kate. At best people might think I've lost my mind. Not to mention this knowledge would put him in real danger. His only defense is he doesn't know anything. For me, I don't leave my lab unless I'm armored and Kate has her own defenses. No one else does.

"Is it trouble between you and Luke?" He stands to lean against the wall and finish his soda. Carlos has always been a good friend, ever since we were sixteen. If anyone deserves to know, it's him.

But deserves got nothing to do with it.

Instead, I get the bright idea to tell him about my pet project.

"No, really. Luke and I are fine, though we haven't spent nearly enough time together lately."

"Where is the hombre?"

"Him, Fleet, and Perfect are on a special mission for the Governor. She flew to DC for a conference and took the boys as a special security detail. Show the flag, so-to-speak."

He nods. "So what's on your mind then?"

"Artemis," I lie. I hate lying to him. Add another grievance I am going to extract in flesh from the person responsible for all of my pain.

"I don't follow?"

I pull the breaks off and roll over to my computer screen, waving at the second of three monitors. Epic senses the movement and brings it to life. The screen lights up with a video of Earth from orbit.

"I've seen this channel," Carlos says as he walks over to lean on the desk, "Anyone can tune into the camera on the ISS."

"Oh, this isn't ISS. Epic, zoom."

The image blurs and we're looking at a slightly angled image of Phoenix. Another blur and the image shifts to our HQ.

"Pop the window," I order. The metal storm shutter creeks up as the image of our HQ on the video does the same.

"Holy crap!" Carlos runs to the window. He opens the glass and sticks his head out, hand frantically waving in the air. Looking back over his shoulder so he can see himself.

"You have your own spy satellite? That can't be legal..."

I start to respond then stop, it never occurred to me it might be illegal. I know there's a treaty against weapons in space, but that's for governments.

"I'm not sure if it is legal, but what country's laws am I violating? It's space, I'm pretty sure it's past the twelve-mile limit," I say with a grin.

"That is frickin cool!"

The door slides open, revealing Kate and Glacier. Carlos spins around so fast he loses his balance

Stepping sideways, he tries to recover and ends up driving himself into the beanbag chair he favors for playing games.

I shake my head, Kate rolls her eyes and Glacier *giggles*. I couldn't be more surprised at the ice queen if she suddenly turned human.

"Hi," Carlos says from his half-fallen, half-laying position on the bag.

"Suave," I say. I'm actually glad he fell. I don't want anyone else knowing about Artemis and I haven't had the chance to tell Kate. I may never have to use her but if I do, I want it to be a surprise. You can't defend against what you can't see coming.

Kate throws a glance my way, an eyebrow quirking up. Crap. She can probably sense my desire to keep Artemis hidden. I flip the monitor off and rely on Epic to take care of the rest. The window closes and the shutter rolls down into place.

"Carlos, this is Glacier, she's the newest member."

Carlos scrambles up pulling his shirt down and takes his 'cool' stance before muttering a 'hey' at our resident ice elemental. To my utter surprise, she actually smiles at him and does a little wave. I can tell it's caught Kate off guard too, she gives them both a look before returning to me.

"Amelia, you mind if we talk for a moment?"

"Sure, Carlos can you show Glacier the break room?"

He stands up straight like he's just been ordered to protect the Queen of England, "Of course. Uhm, I guess you probably don't eat, huh?"

Good one Carlos, stick that foot right in your mouth.

"No," she shakes her head. "You can call me Monica," she says. Carlos walks over to join her. I can't really read her expression, the ice moves exactly as human flesh would, but being partially see-through makes it impossible to read the minutia.

"Well, then maybe I can interest you in a game of foosball?"

"You're on," she says as they walk out together.

"Should I be jealous?" Kate asks after the two leave.

"Maybe?" Kate isn't serious, of course. Carlos, like virtually every other man in her life, crushes hard on her. But as she told me, it isn't her, it's her powers. Part of being an empath is everyone feels a connection to her, even if she doesn't reciprocate. It just so happens my armor protected me when we first met. Our friendship is actually a friendship. It's why she could teleport to me shortly after we met. Something that normally takes weeks or even months of knowing a person.

"Two things," Kate says as she slides her shapely bottom onto my desk, "Any progress on Glacier? I know she's hard to read but she really has built up some hope that you're the real deal."

I wheel myself back and spin around to my research station. I have the lab set up in parts. Armor maintenance, utility, and active research. Utility covers Artemis and just about anything I'm actively doing that isn't the other two. My research station is farthest from the door and the most powerful quantum computer I've ever built. After I transferred Epic out of his housing and into the armor I re-purposed his old case as a research machine.

"She's interesting, that's for sure. You know about the Tesla waves right? The catch-all name for the other-dimensional energy scientist theorize you supers use?"

"Sure, that's the thing they figured out after World War Two? Right?"

"Head of the class," I mutter as I tap a few keys. What I wouldn't give for a holographic interface like she has on her phone, but I will be damned if I allow any Cat-7 gear in my lab. And that kind of tech is slightly outside my bailiwick. Everything in here is something I've built myself, or had custom manufactured for my shell company, Mars Tech Global.

"Well when you or any super aren't actively using your powers your Tesla waves look something like this," I pull up a scan of Kate from a couple of months back. Epic needed a detailed biometric map of her for security reasons. The image of her body fluctuates in many different colors. With the punch of a key, I highlight the Tesla waves. They're there, but faint.

"Now, if you use your powers actively," the faint blue energy turns brilliant and blinding.

"Wow," Kate says. She slides off the table and leans over my chair to look closer at the monitor. "How did you find this?"

"Epic. He did the math, I just set the parameters."

"Does anyone else know this?"

"About Tesla waves? Sure, but there isn't anything noteworthy in it. We can't quantify the waves, measure their power or anything other than see the effect they have on our bodies' electromagnetic field."

"So this isn't actually the waves we're looking at."

"Nope. This is a magneto scan of your field. As you exert power your field amps up. Think of a battery. Just sitting there it doesn't really have much going on. But, if you charge it or expend the charge it lights right up."

She nods, "Damn, I thought you were on to something with this. No Nobel prize for you then."

"Ha, as if I want one." I punch a few more keys and throw up a scan of Glacier I did a few days ago. "What do you see?"

"Uh, I'm not sure. Looks like mine."

And it does look like hers... "Except it shouldn't."

She takes her glasses off, pulling the guest chair up next to mine and sitting down, "I don't follow."

A few clicks and I move their EM field to a side by side. "You're a flesh and bone person, Kate. A perfect person, but a person all the same."

She shrugs the compliment off, "Hardly perfect."

"Still, you, me, anyone and everyone has an EM field. Some people naturally have strong ones, some have small ones, but everyone has it."

"Okay, you're telling me she's just like everyone else."

I wait for her to put it together. She's not stupid, despite her public persona, she knows what's what. Her eyes light up as she figures it out. "But she's not like you or me?"

"Bingo. Ice doesn't have an EM field. It's just condensed gas, really. How does she have an EM field if she really is just gas?"

"I don't suppose you know..."

"Not yet," I grin, "But you know how much I like puzzles. We have EM fields because we're physical matter with iron, copper, flesh, and bone. Our brains generate an electrical field that's relayed through our central nervous system. If I had to guess, I would say Monica's body is out there, somewhere. Maybe in whatever dimension the ice comes from. If that is the case, then there has to be a way to bring her back. However, that's something I am nowhere near."

I tap a few more keys and pull up the status of the labs Faraday cage. I'd put one in the whole building but everyone claims they need cell service or some such nonsense. Status is a hundred percent which means our conversation is private. "Okay, shields are up. What is number two?"

She rolls her eyes at my Star Trek reference.

"Your parents. I talked to Dr. Grace, the neurologist in charge of their case." I try not to flinch but it doesn't matter when my best friend is an empath. "It isn't all bad, Amelia," she says in a much lower voice, putting her hand on my shoulder. "The controls on them are pretty sophisticated, but...," she gives me a squeeze, "There's hope. She's confident at least some of it can be undone."

Some of it? What if the 'some' is just regular stuff? What if they never remember having a daughter? What if—my eyes water and I put my head in my hands leaning over as far as I dare. All this time. All this work. And for what? I have two people back who might as well be strangers. A well of depression opens up under me and I feel like I'm falling.

Think, Amelia! Think. Can a telepath be forced to undo his work? Maybe, but then he could just as likely do more damage, and why not? Sure, I know how to block him—maybe—but not everyone can walk around with a ZPFM powered Faraday cage.

"I take it," I say between large breaths, "That a different telepath couldn't really undo the changes, huh? I mean, they could give them new controls, but it would never be more than just another manipulation?"

Kate doesn't answer, I don't need her to, I already know. The only way I get my parents back is if they remember on their own, or I make the person responsible undo the damage.

Which begs the question, how much hurt am I going to have to put on them to make it happen?

"Amelia, I don't like where your feelings are going."

"It's okay, I'm okay. Listen, I think I know what we need to do. How do you feel about a little trip to New York?" I fill her in on my plan along with Artemis and my little side trip to Greece, I don't want there to be any secrets between us. And if there is one person who will believe it's Kate.

"For real? Like, he's a Greek god?" She asks about Sydney.

"No, but he might as well be. You believe me then?"

"Kate, you can't lie to me. Heck, when I'm the room you can't even lie to yourself."

I smile, I knew she would believe me. At least, I hoped.

She leans over and hugs me in a warm embrace "I will always believe you."

15

I leave Carlos knee deep in Halo. He asked if he could hang out for the day and talk to Epic. I know they've spoken in the past about his future, so it isn't a problem. I adore Carlos, next to Kate and Luke he is my only other real friend. He has no prospects, though. He plays guitar, lives with his folks, and works a lousy nine-to-five. He needs a future of his own making and hopefully Epic can get him squared away and on the right path.

In the meantime, I'm on my way to New York. Flying high above the US in a lazy ark. This has got to be the best part about Arsenal—flying!

Incoming call—Major Force.

My whole world lights up. Okay, second best part.

"Luke!"

"Amelia! Oh, it's good to hear your voice. I've only got audio, can you flip on video?"

I navigate through my HUD to the video option and activate the tiny camera looking down at my face. He sees a fishbowl view of me.

"You're in your armor?"

"Yeah, it's a long story but I'm actually..." before I spill I check the signal status. Epic encrypts all our communications but there's always the possibility of a leak. Hmm, maybe I could really launch a comsat with one-hundred percent encryption security—

"Earth to Amelia," he says with a heart-stopping smile.

"Sorry, I had an idea. Listen, I'm actually on my way to New York to check out a lead on about my investigation. Maybe I could swing by on my way back? I've never been to DC."

"You've never been to New York either, is everything okay? You know you don't have any law enforcement authority outside of the State Of Arizona, right?"

"I know. This is just a meet and greet at Kate's old school. Otherwise, I'd inform Nightwatch before going."

Can I tell him the whole story without endangering him? No. The less he knows the better. I shouldn't have even told him where I was, but I really want to see him. I need his arms around me. Sigh. That just isn't going to happen.

"I could have gone commercial but this saves us a couple of days."

I check the clock, currently, it's five p.m. in DC. Maybe another half hour to New York, and an hour there... "I could be there in a few hours, grab a late dinner?"

"No can do, sorry. The Governor is in wall-to-wall meetings until we leave. FBI, Homeland, DMHA, the whole bit. There's some kind of international conference going on and we're here until the very end. We're scheduled to catch a flight back at seven. Late dinner tonight?"

"Of course, see you then."

He looks like he wants to say something but then doesn't. Instead, he smiles and kills the feed.

The rest of the trip I go over what we have so far. Cat-7 is the public face of the Cabal. They probably launder money for them too. If I had to guess, whoever the telepath is will most likely be the true mastermind. Which means no leaving my lab if I'm not in armor. Who knows what he needs to control me. It could be proximity or touch, just about anything.

If only I had a name. With that, I could wrap this all up. No more looking over my shoulder, and I'd have my parents back for real. Just one little name.

The flight doesn't take long. The sun takes a slow dive behind me as we cross the New York state line. The school is up north, far away from any major city... well, far away for the East Coast. I don't know how these people stand being so smooshed together.

We're coming up on the school. I've notified their dispatch. Headmistress Mrudani Mistry will be meeting our arrival.

I land just outside the grounds. I imagine they have some kind of air defense and there's no point in setting it off. The moment my feet touch ground a *pop* of displaced air sounds next to me and Kate walks by as if she were there all along. She's dressed as Domino, mask and all.

The main gate is manned by a single guard whose startled expression has me laughing in my suit. He opens the door to the booth, hand on his sidearm before his eyes go wide.

"Kate?"

"Perry!" She squeals running over to him and throwing her arms around the guard. Now that I have a second I realize he's much older than I thought, at least in his fifties. He's a big man with salt and pepper hair. His uniform is well-kept and he wears it well, despite the spare tire around his waist.

"What are you doing here? We haven't seen you in ages."

She casts her eyes down at the ground, "Sorry Perry. Things in Arizona have been hopping. I really do miss you and the rest of the staff."

He shakes his head, pulling her into another hug, "There there, no worries dear. It's our nature in life. You were a true joy to have around, this school is lesser for your absence. Let me get the gate and I'll walk you to the lobby."

The old gate whirs open and we slip through. Kate chats with him as we make our way up the road. It isn't long to the main building, just long enough for me to scan the grounds. Security is high, lots of cameras, motion sensors, walls and other electronic snoopers.

Not a lot of people, though. Maybe it's just because it's early evening?

Perry opens the main door and ushers us in. The lobby feels like an old house more than a school. Couches and sofas are scattered throughout the room, lots of windows shower us in fading natural light.

"I was sorry to hear about Mr. Kana," she tells the guard. He stiffens for a second before patting her hand.

"Me too. Well, I've got to get back to the gate. Don't stay away so long next time."

"Of course, it was good to see you."

He closes the door behind him leaving us in the room.

"Feel anything out of the ordinary?" I ask her. She glances around the room, her eyes lingering on every couch, every painting.

"I don't know if it is just I've been gone for so long, or *what,* but something feels off."

"You can defend yourself, right? From," I twirl my fingers in the air next to my head.

She smirks, "Yes, I can. I may not be a telepath but I don't need to be for defense. A strong mind is a strong mind."

A faux wooden panel opens and a slim woman in a black suit jacket and skirt walks out. She has her hair in a bun, thick-rimmed black glasses adorn her dark-skinned face. She reminds me of every teacher I've ever had. Not that I had many.

"Ms. Petrenelli, a pleasure to have one of our Alumni back with us." She shakes Kate's hand with a warm smile and then turns to me, "I'm afraid I haven't had the pleasure?"

"I'm Arsenal," I say holding out my armored palm. An awkward shake later and we're walking through the door to her office.

"What brings a former pupil here, Ms. Petrenelli?"

Kate sits in front of the large desk but the chairs are too small for me. I end up standing behind her. The office is nice, faux leather furniture, lots of bookshelf space. The pictures on the walls look like former pupils, whole classes of them. Fifty or sixty years worth of students. Epic scans them all, identifying Kate for me. I can't believe the girl in the photo is the same person before me. The girl looks *hollow*. Dressed in clothes far too large for her. With dark makeup and a hood pulled tight around her face.

"I would like to get in touch with Mr. Kana's family, to pay my respects," Kate tells the headmistress.

I ignore their conversation as I focus on my HUD. "Epic?" I flip through my active sensors. "Is it me or is there hardly anyone here?" I'd thought as much walking up the drive but now that we're in the building I can't detect more than a dozen people.

He takes over, switching between modes and adjusting settings to be as sensitive as possible. After a moment my HUD returns to normal.

There are twelve people on the grounds. They have beds for ten times that. Based on location and patterns I would say almost all of those people are employees. As far as I can tell, they have no students. Which isn't what their public database says.

"Well, that isn't right. I was hoping to avoid this but... oh well, hack their computer. Let's get everything we can."

Working. Their firewall is remarkably primitive and—

"What?"

Beyond the base operating system and the usual things you would expect to find, their computers are blank. No files, no data. Just as they were out of the box. We would need access to a data port for me to find anything deeper.

"Excuse me?" I interrupt, raising my hand. "I need to use the little girl's room..."

Kate raises one delicate eyebrow at me before the headmistress answers, "Out the door, down the hall, third door on the right. Now, Ms. Petrenelli, I'm afraid I can't divulge information—"

I lose track of the conversation when the door closes behind me.

"Okay, I don't really need the bathroom. Do a magnetic scan and find me the hardline."

A wireframe outline of the room replaces my visuals as Epic searches out magnetic fields.

There is an ethernet port underneath the frontdesk.

The desk is empty, no notepads, no telephone, only a computer terminal with one of the useless computers set up to look like it's functional. Kneeling down, I see the port. I don't have time for fancy. The drywall crumbles as I grab the faceplate, crush it and pull. The suit comes into direct contact with the wire, giving us access.

I'm in. The network server is offline. However, they didn't unplug it. Powering on...

"Take your time. I don't look conspicuous at all crouched under a desk."

The servers are wiped. I don't think they degaussed or deleted the hard drives more than a few times. Copying sectors now.

Kate's muffled voice comes through the wall, she'd have to be damn near screaming for me to hear. I can't make out what she's saying but I can certainly tell she's upset. This close to the floor I notice something I didn't coming in. There's a fine layer of dust covering the ground. No one has stood or sat behind this desk in a very long time.

"Any time now..."

There are only a few hundred gigabytes of data. Ten more seconds. Done. I can work on putting the sectors back together after we leave, but Amelia?

"Yeah?

They haven't admitted a new student since Mr. Kana's death.

"Maybe they can't find a strong enough telepath to ride shepherd on the kids?"

Their public record shows them admitting over a hundred empaths and at least twenty telepaths in the intervening years. I can find no internal records of them living here.

"What the hell?"

This stinks to high heaven. A school for mental powers with no students? If a telepath is behind all my problems... Is Mr. Kana really dead? Could he be behind it all, somehow faked his death? That doesn't make sense, though. He died five years ago. My parents went missing long before then.

The door slides open as I walk back in. Kate is standing, leaning over the desk with her finger in Mrs. Mistry's face.

Contaminated atmo detected, switching to internals.

She must really have the juice amped up. They're both screaming at each other. I've never seen Kate so angry.

"You know damn well no mugger killed him. What is the school hiding?"

"I'm afraid you've exceeded your welcome, Domino. Take your guest and leave."

Yeah, that isn't going to happen.

"Where are all the students?" I ask.

Kate turns to look at me then her eyes unfocus the way they do when she's doing her thing.

"I don't know what you mean," Mrs. Mistry replies.

Kate's head snaps around, "You're lying. You can't lie to me. Where are all the students?"

The headmistress opens her mouth to reply then stops, abruptly sitting.

"Why aren't there any students on campus?" Kate demands.

"More importantly, why have you publicly admitted students for the last five years, but none of them are here? Where did they all go?" I ask.

She looks back and forth between the two of us. I can see in her eyes she's afraid. I'm no empath but I know what fear looks like, I've seen it on my own face enough times.

"Listen, you have to understand," she says, patting down her jacket before reaching over to her desk and opening a drawer, "There isn't a lot I can do. I have no—"

She pulls out a large black semi-automatic pistol, places the barrel to her head, and pulls the trigger.

The explosion is deafening in the small room. My audio synthesizers protect me but Kate is left holding her ears. Glass shatters above us followed by a scream and then a person plummets past her office window to land on the sidewalk.

There are gunshots and other sounds of chaos on the campus. I'm not sure what is going on.

"Kate, everyone on campus is committing suicide, we have to leave!"

Her eyes go wide, "Perry?" She runs to the window and vanishes. Her friend, right. If everyone here is programmed to kill themselves if too many questions are asked, then I can only imagine what comes next.

The State Police are en route. I just picked up their signal. A Parker alert has been issued for the school. Two superhumans are rampaging, killing the staff. The Nightwatch is also on the way, ETA three minutes. I think this is a setup, Amelia. Whoever is behind this was waiting for us.

The Nightwatch? New York's super team. If California's team is a joke then they are the exact opposite. We can't tangle with them and something tells me we won't get the chance to explain our side of the situation.

"Epic, Ghost Protocol, wipe everything down."

Two things happen. A canister of aerosolized bleach explodes from my shoulder compartment wiping out any trace Kate was ever here. Then, Epic does his best to wipe all the camera feeds and any other electronic evidence of our visit.

Once outside, I survey the massacre. I only find three bodies, but my thermal readings aren't promising. Kate appears next to me, holding an unconscious Perry. He's bleeding from a grievous head wound. It looks like the bullet creased his skull. She must've gotten to him at the last possible second.

"When I took the gun away he started pounding his head against a brick wall. Who would do this?"

"The same person who took my parents. Can you get him to Seattle? Admit him to the hospital? I get the feeling when he wakes up he will just keep trying."

"Good call. Want me to come back for you?"

"No, I'll fly back. I need some time to think anyway. Meet you back home."

She nods and vanishes.

Thirty seconds.

"Stealth mode, lock up and lift off."

I have Epic put us on a ballistic course back to Phoenix. I need time to think so we keep it just above Mach Two. According to the clock, it will take a little under an hour and a half to get home. That's fine with me. There's so much to process I don't even know where to begin. Not to mention the fact that I'm exhausted.

Either someone has been killing telepaths and empaths or making them disappear, one or the other. Knowing our enemy is one, gives me a couple of theories about what has happened to the missing students. Right at the top is competition. Maybe when a telepath is strong enough they can sense others? The way Kate sparred with Sam Sykes, her powers were stronger so she won.

Why maintain the school then? Why not just have... well, I'm stupid.

"Epic, search for everyone who has publicly gone to the school since Mr. Kana's death. Are they anywhere else?"

Negative. Once they go to the school their public record vanishes. Amelia, upon further research I'm not sure anyone telepath would have sufficient strength for this. Even if he or she were capable of remote control... There were hundreds of students. Each with family and friends. None of them have ever been reported missing or so much as a 911 call made. This would require many telepaths to perform this level of alteration.

"You're saying we're not dealing with one rogue telepath but several... great. How many would it take to do this efficiently?"

At least twenty. All F4 or F5. With a high probability that there are more than that.

"Are there that many on record?"

Negative. As Kate said, there are not many F5 telepaths. Mr. Kana was one, Mariposa of the Brigade is another. There are four others in the entire world. A half dozen F4s and thirty-one F3s.

"I don't suppose it's possible that almost the entire world's population of telepaths are in some kind of secret society? We already know whoever's masterminding this wants world domination. And according to Pythia, that's exactly what they will get."

The Oracle said she saw two futures. One where we cause the end and one that is despotism and slavery. While one telepath could conceivably hold the world together, a group of them could do it easily. While there is most certainly one person in charge it would appear that we are—

"We're fighting an army, great."

It would seem so.

"An army of telepaths who control one of the largest companies in the world, have their hands in multiple supervillains and are bent on world domination. This isn't 1938, Epic. Who wants to control the world anymore?"

I do not have enough data to suggest motive.

"Me neither," I sigh.

The lights of Kansas City pass below. The interactive map pings the halfway point.

"Okay, I'm going to try and sleep, wake me up when we need to start our approach."

Closing my eyes I try to push out all the terrible visions of the future. Pythia said there wasn't a future if I continued my *crusade,* as she called it. Not that humanity would be hurt, but simply had no future. This is the stuff of nightmares and sleep doesn't come.

Five minutes out. I am contacting Phoenix ATC for clearance. Carlos left you a message that he has returned home and will see you tomorrow. Luke is waiting for you at HQ with dinner. Kate made it to Seattle safe and sound. She is staying there for a day to make sure her friend is okay. ATC has given us clearance, follow the yellow brick road.

A yellow path highlights on my HUD with speed and maneuvering directions, when to slow down, and when to turn. The thrusters cut and gravity takes over with the occasional assist from my stabilizers. No need to fight momentum when wind resistance and friction do the work for me.

Once I'm down under three hundred feet I use direct thrust and slow down even more. Phoenix flashes under me in a colorful chorus of lights and sounds. I'm not a huge fan of going out in the city at night. From this high up, though, it's breathtaking.

Coming up on—Amelia—we have guests. I am sorry I did not see them sooner, they must have been jamming.

My HUD clears of the ATC directions and shows the HQ. On the other side of the parking lot is a familiar looking VTOL. The Brigade loiters around beneath the wing while Captain Freedom and Luke speak a few feet away. Epic tags everyone with identifiers.

Freedom, the hockey-mask-wearing super soldier. Torque, forcefield generation. Comanche, directed energy beams. *Mariposa*... flight and telepathy. Behemoth, invulnerability, and strength.

A hundred feet out I spot their escort, six bipedal robots painted with army camo, each with a plasma gun for an arm.

That would answer the question on Mariposa. We should assume the Brigade is under the control of our antagonist and act accordingly.

"Roger that, buddy. However, I don't want to see the team get hurt... let's see what is what. Just to be on the safe side let's put ECM to max."

I land hard a few feet from Luke, sending up a plume of dust. Mr. Perfect, Fleet, and Glacier are in costume and hanging back, which speaks volumes for this visit.

I glance at Mariposa, she's fluttering around by the aircraft behind her team, she doesn't take her eyes off me while I walk toward Freedom.

Our Faraday cage is catching interference.

The metallic ink on the outside of the armor glitters like diamonds in a spotlight. So much for this being a friendly visit.

"Captain Freedom, good to see you again," I say coming to a halt next to Luke. My boyfriend doesn't look happy. He flashes a worried glance at me as I speak.

"Arsenal, I'm afraid we're going to need you to come with us. Please take off the armor and..."

I hold up my hand. "Hold up the horses skipper. I'm not going anywhere with anyone and I'm certainly not going to take off my armor. Care to explain what this is about?"

Then, to Epic, "Broad spectrum ECM, let's make sure Mariposa doesn't take control of our friends."

As if he were completely prepared he pulls out a tablet and holds it up for me. The video playing is shaky and grainy at best. It shows a building, the one from Boston, and a dark figure crashing into the roof.

After several enhancements the dark figure takes form and it *could* be me. I know it is, but they don't, not for sure.

Then the image shifts to New York. It shows me and Kate entering the school then the next shot is of us leaving, her with Perry and me by myself. The screen shifts showing eleven bodies in various states of death.

"We're arresting you for the destruction of private property and the suspected murder of eleven people. Not to mention the kidnapping of a security guard. If you tell us where Domino is, this will go easier on you."

I'm the dumbest smart person in the world. I was so fixated on stopping whoever's behind this, I didn't think about them being ready for me legally. They couldn't get their grubby hands on my armor illegally so they just waited and watched for me to step outside the law. They must have hidden cameras in New York, knowing I would go there. And then I dragged Kate into it. Epic warned me it was a setup, I should have taken more precautions.

Awesome.

"Listen, Freedom, there is a perfectly innocent explanation for this, I—"

"This is you, not some trick?" Luke asks. The hurt on his face is plain. My heart constricts in my chest. As if I didn't have enough going on.

"Luke, I found a lead to who took my parents."

"That's great but why didn't you tell me?"

"Every piece of evidence," and I say this to both of them while glancing at the butterfly-winged woman thirty feet away, "Suggests there is a telepath behind it. If I told you anything they would be able to read your thoughts and without knowing who it was... I didn't want you to be in danger just for knowing."

Luke nods, I can see he understands when he puts his hand on my shoulder.

Freedom interrupts, "That aside, you broke the law, Arsenal. I need you to take off the armor and come with me."

"You know I can't do that. In here I'm safe, once it's off, there's nothing stopping Fluttershy over there from controlling me the way her boss controlled my parents."

That makes him pause. She reacts, even though she doesn't have super hearing. She must be riding shotgun in his mind and then I know the jig is up.

Freedom takes a swing at Luke. His powers kick in and he steps back a heartbeat before it connects.

"Diamondbacks, protect Arsenal!" Luke shouts.

We are seriously outgunned.

"Thrusters, we need distance," I yell. Epic tags everyone as we climb. The one I'm most worried about is—

Alarms scream as we slam into the ground. My HUD blares red as outside pressure increases ten-fold.

Localized gravity increase.

"Fleet, take out Torque. Mr. Perfect, engage Mariposa, keep her off balance so she can't use her mind control powers."

I'm guessing it's probably hard enough for her to maintain control of her own team let alone break through the ECM to take over mine.

"On it," Fleet says.

"As you wish," Mr. Perfect replies.

The gravity field lets up almost immediately. Rolling over, I see Fleet holding Torque with both hands as he spins in a circle fast enough to create a small tornado.

Comanche steps forward and fires off his twin ion beams. Tommy vanishes in a swirl of dust reappearing a few feet away to throw a rock at him. Torque sails off in the distance and I don't envy his landing.

An ice blue hand reaches down to help me up.

"I don't know you and I don't know your team. But, do you really think you can help me?" Glacier asks.

"I do," I say, as she pulls me up.

"Then I'm on your side, what do you want me to do?"

I glance around at the battle. Luke and Freedom are going toe-to-toe, Perfect is keeping Mariposa busy with his constructs, and Tommy has Torque down for the count leaving Comanche and Behemoth... who doesn't seem to be doing anything? Just leaning against the plane as if she doesn't have a care in the world.

"If Mariposa has a free second, she'll mind control you. Keep her busy?"

Glacier grins and skates off behind Perfect before sending out jets of ice at the fluttering telepath.

Torque drags himself up from the truck that stopped his momentum. We can't have that. Three bean bags hit him in the chest with the force of a car crash. He falls face down.

Comanche rakes his eyebeams across the field toward me.

"Floor it!"

Comanche and the four robots are firing wildly trying to score a hit. I know the plasma weapons will take me out, I'm not sure about Comanche's ion beams though.

"Epic, find me a targeting solution for the four robots. We know a shot through the chest will finish them. Let's set it up like pins."

Affirmative.

Green balls of death fly through the air and I get the feeling the robots aren't trying to kill me so much as keep me from fleeing.

Twin ion beams of white-hot fire flash through the sky. A sign explodes, followed by a car. I have to stay low or he'll just flash over me. As long as he might hit his team he'll be careful.

I fire off a couple of bean bags at Comanche but he just vaporizes them. I'm too far away for the IP Cannons and I don't want to kill him. Maybe I can take out two birds with one stone.

Robots, hard left, plant and fire.

I do it. I come to a crashing halt. Lift my arms and the moment they line up Epic fires. The hyper-accelerated silicate rips through two of them setting off secondary explosions.

"Luke, King's Gambit." We have our own comms and he hears me. We've worked on moves before and this one is tricky. I leap into the air at full acceleration.

"Epic, ready the kinetic field..."

Ready.

I accelerate hard, in the limited space available. He steps back from Freedom with a kick that lands on his chest. Reaching out to me, we lock hands and I slam feet first into the ground. Epic triggers my kinetic field to simulate a few thousand pounds so I have far more mass than normal and we spin. Using my momentum and Luke's, we manage one full rotation before I let go. Like a human missile, he flies right at Comanche.

The Brigade member held off his ion beams when I got close to Freedom and now he's unprepared for the hit. Luke crashes with the force of a truck. I can hear bones breaking from here. But what can I do? The man's powers are deadly. It's either hurt him or kill him. Mind-controlled or not I don't feel like murdering people who think they're doing right.

A size twelve boot hits me in the head with staggering force.

"Freedom, listen. You're being mind-controlled. Mariposa isn't on the side of justice here, she's manipulating you."

He shakes his head, "You're the one on the wrong side, Arsenal. You just don't know it yet. Behemoth, end this."

"Epic, brace for—"

Behemoth grins as she pushes herself off the plane, arms out wide she leaps forward and slaps her hands together.

The thunderclap ripples before her, obliterating the ground and throwing everyone off their feet. The shock wave slams into Tommy, knocking him to the ground. Luke leaps in front of Glacier to take the brunt of it. Mr. Perfect slamms into a car crumpling like so much tissue paper. The remaining two robots explode as the shock ripples through the air.

The force wave rolls harmlessly over me since we still had our kinetic field set to root us in the ground. When the dust clears only Tommy and I are standing. Their team still has Freedom, Behemoth, and Mariposa.

"You're tougher than you look," Behemoth growls.

Pierre and Luke are in serious condition. Both are unconscious and have sustained life-threatening wounds. Glaciers status is unknown.

This is not how I imagined the day going. Behemoth alone is all but unbeatable, but now it's me against their three most experienced members.

"Is anyone up?"

"Arsenal, I got some distance when Behemoth did her thing. What do you want me to do?" Fleet asks.

As fast as he is, he can't turn the tide, but he can save Luke and Pierre.

"Evac the wounded, then Glacier."

"Roger."

"Glacier," she turns to me when I speak, her body is filled with spider web cracks from the sonic attack. If Luke hadn't leaped in front of her, she would be dead. "Freeze that big piece of crap."

"With pleasure."

The blue girl rolls her ice shoulders and slaps her hands together not unlike the move Behemoth did. Freedom and Mariposa are still recovering from the friendly fire when blue light flashes from Glacier's palms and strikes Behemoth dead center. The woman howls and starts marching forward, each foot falling with the force of a small earthquake.

"Epic, pod Freedom, go full automated attack against Mariposa, we can't let her control anyone while Tommy gets the team to safety."

Affirmative. Amelia, the jig is up and the lab is lost... do you want me to enact Enterprise Refit protocol?

Dammit, no I don't. A quick glance at the situation tells me that no matter how this turns out, I'm done with the Diamondbacks.

"Do it."

Verbal confirmation code required.

"Zero-zero-zero-destruct-zero."

Glacier pours on the power but Behemoth is somehow closing ground. The *puff* off my launcher signals Epic going after Freedom. Mariposa is on the ground fifty feet away. She's shaking her head trying to clear it from the shockwave her teammate smacked her with.

Initiating fire alarm. All personnel are evacuating.

The suit bucks as I slam into the ground next to the butterfly-winged woman. I've never really looked at her before but I see it now, she's beautiful in an elegant way. Everyone in the media is always going on about how wonderful she is. To me, she's just another despot trying to take over the world.

I snag her tunic and lift her off the ground.

"If you so much as flinch I will shatter every bone in your face, understand?"

She nods and her eyes snap open, clearing of confusion immediately. The shield on my gloves sparkle like a live wire has arced against it.

"I've developed defenses to your powers, they won't work on me. You people... it never occurs to you that if you can do it, so can I. Now give me a name!"

She shakes her head, "You don't understand, Amelia. We're trying to save the world."

"I don't care what brand of crazy you are. Tell me who's in charge, a name Mariposa, I want a name. Who messed with my parents' minds?"

I shake her to focus her thoughts. If she so much as glances away from me I'm blasting her with my kinetic lance. At point blank range it will likely shatter her face.

Building evacuation confirmed. Safeties off Artemis is locked on. Adjusting orbital parameters...

"Arsenal, Force, and Perfect are in the hospital what next?"

"Tommy, get Glacier out of here. You two lay low for a few days. I'll contact you and let you know where to go from there."

"Amelia, we're not leaving you," he says.

Mariposa smiles as if she can read my thoughts, but I know she can't. She thinks I'm being indecisive, the truth is I'm multi-tasking.

"Tommy, seriously. There's a lot going on here you don't know. I need you two to vanish for a few days, can you do that?"

"What about helping me? You promised," Glacier asks.

Epic shows Behemoths progress on the split screen. The monstrosity that is the unstoppable woman takes one earth-shattering step after another. Glacier is visibly weakening and I'm out of time.

MKI Arrow locked. Firing in seven seconds.

"Monica, I will. I know I can, it will just take some time. Go with Tommy and I will explain when I can."

I put my full attention back on Mariposa.

She glowers at me, "They can't hide from me, you know. Or from us. We're everywhere. Controlling everyone who matters. You only slipped through our net because we thought you were dead. *He* thought you were dead. You're only one woman, Amelia. You can't outsmart all of us..."

"The hell I can't," I fire the kinetic lance. I let the energy carry her away from me in a vortex of broken bones and blood. She crumples to the ground a few feet away. She's going to need serious plastic surgery if she ever wants to show her face in public again. The life signs on my HUD tell me she'll live. I'm tempted not to let her. They're building a world where life and happiness mean nothing. I can't fight against that by being like them, so she lives.

Glacier vanishes in a blur of speed as Tommy carries her to safety.

"Epic, make sure they're taken care of. Divert funds from Mars if you have to. Legal and everything. I don't want any of this coming back on the team."

Affirmative.

With Glacier no longer actively freezing Behemoth she is free to come after me. Freedom is floating up into the sky trying to contort himself to reach the AG pod on his back.

In the pipe.

I nod. The ground shakes as the massive woman sprints toward me. I feel like a herd of elephants are bearing down on me. I fire off full IP cannons just in case as I blast off. The blue energy envelopes her and flashes down to the ground with no effect. Just like White Rhino and every other invulnerable person I've fought.

She can't fly, but she can throw things at me. I just need a little time. I check the clock.

On the way.

Thirty seconds until impact. I fly to the building, Behemoth tosses everything from cars to robot parts at me. I land in front of the main doors. I know what's coming and I try not to think of my Xbox. My game collection is digital but still, it pains me to know I'm about to trash it all.

Holding my arms out wide Epic triggers my PA, "I'm right here, Bitchamoth. Come at me bro."

"Like I've never heard that one before. You know what's wrong with you. You think you're smarter than everyone else. You think you have it all figured out and no one could possibly be one step ahead of you."

She's not wrong. I do have that problem. Reinforced by the fact that I'm almost always right.

"You know you're being manipulated right? There's someone controlling your thoughts and motivations. He's controlling everyone and when he's done this isn't a world any of us are going to want to live in," I tell her.

She shakes her head, "This is what I mean. You think that given the facts any decent person would agree with you." She's walking calmly forward as she speaks, not at all angry or raging the way Luke does. "But that isn't true. Can't you imagine being shown the end of humanity and then deciding to do whatever it takes to stop the coming destruction? There's something coming, something you can't fathom. And we're the answer, Amelia. We're the next step. If you *knew* that a billion people were going to die tomorrow and all you had to do to save them was kill a few million, wouldn't you? You're the math genius, right? Tell me the numbers."

It's the ultimate catch-22. Do you kill one life to save two? She's close now, only ten feet away but she doesn't look like she's going to attack.

"The only problem with that calculation is you don't have all the variables. You aren't killing people to save lives, you're killing people on the *chance* it will save lives. You're trying to stop something awful by being awful. What does it matter if we win if there's nothing left that makes us human?"

"It only matters that we win," she says. She towers over me, standing this close. She could reach out and crush this suit like a discarded soda can if it weren't for my shields.

"That's the difference between us, Behemoth. For me, it matters how I win."

She grins, "The difference between you and me is I'm alive and you're not." She reaches out in a heartbeat and grabs my helmet with both hands. The alarms scream from the pressure. The ZPFM kicks into overdrive flooding power into my kinetic shields keeping her fingers only inches from my skull.

"No, Behemoth, the difference between you and me is I'm right and you're wrong. Also, yeah, I'm smarter than you."

Her eyes go wide when the suit doesn't pop. If it were just the metal she would totally break me in half. But with the kinetic shields powered by a ZPFM, I'm a lot stronger and tougher than she thinks. Still, I can't stand here forever. I plant a foot in her gut and throw myself backward with an Emdrive assisted heave. I've read she can manipulate her mass. However, she isn't ready for this. Epic slams me back and to the ground using both the kinetic emitters to temporarily adjust my weight and the Emdrive to 'push' us back. She flips over me and crashes upside down into the building, turning the entryway into a symphony of shattering glass and rending steel.

"Up!"

Three seconds.

"Full burn."

The Emdrive kicks in and I see Behemoth crawling out of the debris just as a strobing yellow light flashes down lighting the whole area.

I didn't name Artemis on a whim. Not only is she a spy satellite, but she also carries twenty-four osmium filled tungsten carbide 'arrows'. Dropped, not launched. They hit the earth at five miles per second with the force of three thousand pounds of TNT.

The arrow burns through the air leaving a trail of ionized gas behind before striking the Diamondbacks HQ. The flash lights up the sky and the entire building is consumed in a massive fireball that rockets hundreds of feet into the air.

I'm a half mile away when it happens and I can feel the force wave pass over me. The mushroom cloud climbs high into the night fading as the wind carries the debris away.

Where are we going?

"Stealth mode, let's go see a friend one last time."

I try not to look back. I almost succeed.

I n full stealth mode, the MKII is all but invisible. If I
stay under three hundred feet and keep my speed at
a few hundred miles an hour nothing can detect our
passage. Which is exactly what I do as I head East
toward my old neighborhood. I never sold the house; I
had planned on giving it away. Of course, that is the
first place they'll look, so there is no point in going.
However, a few houses down should be safe, for a while
at least.

Epic goes over the lowdown for me while we fly
to Carlos' house. No casualties, though the Brigade is
seriously hurt. Currently, the news is blaming me for
the explosion saying I was working on an unauthorized
reactor experiment. They're right, I did cause it and no

just the arrow. My investigation into Cat-7 and the Cabal is what brought the Brigade down on us. I shouldn't have been surprised when they did it legally. Whoever is behind this mess is certainly forward thinking. I feel like they're just out of my grasp. Regardless, they're close to an end game. They wouldn't be making moves like this if they weren't.

I pull up the footage of the aftermath of our fight. The news has a spectacular shot of a very naked Behemoth crawling out of the crater my arrow made. I didn't think it would kill her, but damn she's tough. The rest of the team was rushed to the local hospital. The Governor is on TV demanding to know why the federal team was in Arizona without her permission. Interesting.

I have Epic check the hospital, I can't risk calling in case they're watching communications. Pierre and Luke doing fine. Good thing too, if Luke was hurt badly or killed... I don't even want to think of that.

Our destination is ahead.

"Thanks, buddy, land us in his backyard."

I come down in the sandy yard full of discarded toys and sun-bleached lawn furniture. The suit's propulsion doesn't make any noise but there is a plume of dust when I hit the ground.

I text Carlos.

In your backyard. Come out.

What?

Come outside and bring a Coke.

A minute later I'm awkwardly leaning against the side of the house with my faceplate up. I hadn't realized how thirsty I was until I asked him to bring a drink. It isn't easy to put anything in my mouth, the helmet wraps around my chin and face to make sure an impact doesn't spin the armor around. However Carlos is very thoughtful and brought a straw.

"I saw the news, damn, niña, was that your satellite or did you build a nuclear weapon into the suit?"

I snort, trying to swallow the soda before it goes out my nose. "Funny, no it's the satellite. Kind of an emergency backup if I ever had to destroy something down to the foundation."

"Can you use it again or is it a one-shot?"

"Assuming Cat-7 hasn't pinpointed the orbit, and I won't know until tomorrow, I can use it again. Right now Artemis is in stealth mode, folded up to make herself smaller. On top of that, I used the latest infrared and radar absorbent paint to keep her invisible. I did a lot of math to make sure her orbit wouldn't put anything in danger up there nor would she collide with the twenty-thousand something pieces of debris floating around."

He smiles taking a pull from his own Coke. "Well, you surely did it. I take it this means you know who's behind all this?" He asks with a wave of his hands.

"Not yet, I mean, I know what. But I don't have a name yet. I'm close though."

"Too bad there isn't a directory, like a Facebook for bad guys—"

A directory... of course there's a directory. "Carlos, you're a genius!" He looks nervously at the house when I shout.

"How so?"

"I can't go into it, but I promise you I couldn't have figured it out without your help."

"Is there anything I can do? I don't have powers and I'm not a super spy or anything. But if I can help..." He's sweet to ask and I wish there was... wait there is.

"Can you go to Maricopa County General, check on Luke, Pierre, and Monica?" His stature perks up at the mention of the ice queen. "Let them know I'm alright and I'll contact them as soon as I can. Let Luke know..." I want to say more but I just don't know what I would tell Luke.

Carlos puts his hand on my shoulder, "It's okay, I'll tell him."

"Thanks, amigo, I appreciate it. Close faceplate." I hand him the Coke as the suit pressurizes.

"Amelia, will I see you again?"

"I sure hope so. If not, you've been a good friend—"

"None of that. You owe me a rematch on Halo, so you better make it through this." I can see in his eyes what his Hispanic upbringing won't let him say.

I step back off the porch, lock up and blast off.

There is a warrant out for your arrest, publicly now. A Parker alert has been issued in all fifty states plus Puerto Rico. You have even made it to the top of the FBI's most wanted list. Well done.

"They want to stop me and since they have total control of the government they will use any means necessary. That's okay though, because Carlos gave me an idea."

May I inquire as to your brilliant plan?

"We can't extract Shai-Hulud because they'll shut him down before we could get anything useful, right?"

That is correct.

"However, if we were in physical contact with a network hub he had access to..."

Then we could transfer the data far quicker than they could counter. Excellent thought. The only problem is we do not know where a data center is.

"Don't we, though?"

Portland?

"Portland. Seriously, you never actually thought they would build those awesome underground bases for state militias, right? There had to be another reason. I think they're the network. They have teleporters, total access to the teams, heck they could have telepaths down there at any given moment playing 'Invasion of the Body Snatchers' on people and no one would ever know. We break in, steal the info, and get out. If we do it now, they shouldn't even have time to prepare for us."

How do you suggest we get in? You vaporized the Arizona entrance.

Vaporized... yes I did. I can't help but smile at the thought.

"There are four bases that we know of, Portland, Montana, Florida, and DC... but every state militia has an entrance."

Montana is out unless you are planning to attack the UltraMax. So is DC.

"Florida is too far away, that leaves just Portland. Since I don't want to fly to Seattle that leaves only one other team."

Which is the team with the highest probability of having their asses kicked by you...

"Bingo, California it is. Set a course, keep stealth mode on."

Course set. Stealth mode directive still in play.

"Engage!"

Los Angeles is almost due west of us. We fly low over the Joshua Tree national forest, then Palm Dessert. I have to keep it under three hundred feet, which limits me to sub-sonic speeds. Which is still pretty darn fast. Five hundred miles an hour and we're past Riverside and looking at the outskirts of L.A. and it isn't even two in the morning yet.

"I'm gonna need a rest after this. Do you have our mobile lab going yet?"

Almost. Should be ready by the time we return to Phoenix.

It isn't anything fancy, just a semi-truck with everything I need to take off and put on the armor. Plus a bed, food, spare clothing and a medkit. I had it set up as a contingency but I don't actually know how it works. I let Epic do the legwork. This way if anyone was able to read my mind they wouldn't know where it was or anything about it other than the fact that I had one.

We turn south as LA approaches; I want to skirt LAX. Risking a collision with a jumbo jet isn't worth the extra time I would save.

The So-Cal team has their base on the water in Long Beach. I just hope not too many of them are home this time of night.

"Can you remotely connect to their computer?"

I've been trying. They have a very effective DMZ. I will need physical contact.

"That's the plan."

California's official team HQ is a ten-story ode to modern architecture. Shiny, mirror-like windows, curving walls, and lots of round corners dominate the surface. The roof is our best bet with its open-air helipad and elevator.

"Once we pop up to land on the roof we're likely going to be on their sensors. Bear that in mind."

Affirmative.

"Here we go." The building rushes up at me, the city behind reflecting off the mirror like windows. I kill the jets as we pass the eighth floor and let momentum carry us the remaining distance to land on the helipad with a crunch. I've taken two steps when a rush of air and a familiar blur of speed materializes in front of me.

I've only ever met him once, but even if Kate didn't hate this guy I wouldn't like him. Maybe if he didn't have overly tanned skin with shoulder length stark white hair I wouldn't think he was a douche, but with his cocksure grin, I just want to punch him in the face.

"Arsenal. The rest of the team is on the way. We were alerted to your presence the moment you landed. Surrender and we'll go easy on you," he says with false swagger.

"You do know I just single-handedly whooped the Brigade and sent them packing with their tail between their legs, right?"

His costume is a ridiculous green and brown leotard which looks more designed to show off his physique then actually protect him.

"The Brigade is all for show. We're the real deal." He slaps his hands together. A wall of force erupts from him passing harmlessly over me. When the air disturbance ends there are three of him standing shoulder to shoulder. Well, two standing, one floating a foot off the ground.

Reminder: our only less-than-lethal option is the IP Cannons.

"I'm warning you guys, I don't have a lot of time here. There's a lunatic with mind control powers and he's trying to take over the world. All I need is five minutes access to the Portland base and I can find out who he is."

"What? So you can blow up Portland like you did Phoenix?" The flying one asks.

"Fine, be that way." I hold my hands out, palms up, and he hesitates. The sandpaper staccato of my cannons rips through the air. The speedster vanishes and the strong one leaps into the blast to take it. He twitches and drops to one knee, but doesn't go down.

Even if we proceed to lethal options, it is likely they will delay us long enough for the rest of the team to arrive.

Flying-guy zooms into the sky at incredible speeds. He has to have a certain level of invulnerability to turn that sharp at speed.

"If we plugged into their buildings network could you use that to activate the quantum teleporter?"

Do you even need to ask?

"Call Kate," I say as I take to the skies. The jig is up, so I cut stealth mode bringing full power to the shields. Triple Threat clearly trains hard. He works as a team, trying to contain me. Speedy hurls about a thousand marbles at me constantly keeping the barrage up from a hundred different angles to distract me. Flyboy has a cudgel made of a stiff metal. He zooms in close, swinging for the fences each time. The second I stop moving Strongman throws a hundred pound weight at me with the force of a bullet.

Connecting to her cell.

I let out a double blast, narrow beam at maximum power. Strongman drops like a stone this time, the second weight he was about to throw at me rolls aside like a discarded beach ball.

"Amelia?" Kate's melodic voice sounds in my ear.

"Kate, I'm sorry I dragged you into this," I say as I spin to put my arm up and ward off the cudgel.

"You didn't drag me into anything, this was already happening. I'm sorry about Phoenix, I wish I—"

"Listen, no time for that right now. I'm trying to break into the Portland underground. I'm in LA and I could use some help."

There's a moment of silence and I wonder for a second if I misjudged her. Maybe this was one step too far for someone who'd played by the Rules her whole life. Even if the Rules were a lie made up by evil people.

"I need thirty seconds. Please don't be high up when I come in."

"You got it," I say. Thank God. Even with everything I've invented I'm just one person. Unless I want to start killing innocent people, I can't do this alone.

"Epic, ETA on the rest of their team?"

LAX ATC has their hoverbikes two minutes out. However, that could change.

"As soon as Kate arrives, full ECM." I land next to the door, switch to widespread and go to full auto on the cannons. The air fills with their roar as the energy creates a cone of ion pulses. It isn't as effective when I use them this way. However the side effect is the ions in the air become saturated setting up a sort of temporary field. As long as I keep the energy pouring in it's almost like a stun shield.

"Epic, full power to the kinetic shields and go wide angle. I want a large enough area to shield Kate."

Got it.

The kinetic emitters reconfigure to their wedge shape with a hundred percent of the power facing forward to deflect the projectiles to the side. Flying-guy comes in hard and hits the stun field. Ionic energy zaps him out of the air like a bug. The speedy one is all that remains, he plays safe and continues to throw a thousand marbles a second. What makes it through the stun field simply falls flat as it hits the kinetic field.

There's a pop behind me as Domino arrives. She's in costume mask and all, wearing more weapons than I've ever seen her carry.

"Get the door," I yell over my shoulder.

ECM to full. Broad-spectrum jamming has commenced.

I check the load out on my HUD. No 'nades, but I have one EMP, two IR smoke canisters, flares, and all my lethals.

"Doors open."

"Pop smoke."

The cannister ejects from my bulky shoulders, exploding in a shower of purple smoke. I let up on the cannons and back in behind Kate. Once I'm through, I slide the door shut and spot weld it with a half second stream from my Particle Beam.

"What now?" she asks.

"You've been here before, where's their entrance?"

"This way," she says. Domino leaps down the stairs four at a time then crossing the stairwell, bouncing from one landing to the next, her feet never touching the stairs as she leapfrogs back and forth. Lucky for me the stairs are far enough apart that I can lower myself down the center by using enough thrust to slow the fall down to just ten feet per second.

The bottom floor comes up fast and the second I touch down Kate pops in front of me, mid-stride toward the elevator. By the time I catch up she has the control panel off and the wiring exposed.

"Can Epic override it?"

"He did before." I reach in and grab a fistful of wires. No time for finesse.

Accessing restricted controls. The teleporter in Portland is online and connected. I've written a sub-routine to override their local controls.

The door ping their arrival as they slide open. In the elevator I go, Kate tries to crowd in behind me but hold up my arm in place.

"Listen, right now you're just wanted on suspicion. Those morons won't be able to stick anything to you. If you come down you're done for You'll be lucky just to go to jail."

She shakes her head, "Regardless of if th government says I can or can't, this is what I dc Arsenal. This is my job and I'm good at it. I stop th bad guys. Now, quit wasting time."

She vanishes and reappears behind me pressing the 'restricted access' button that leads to the underground. The doors slide silently shut and the elevator hums as it descends.

"You know, at our trial, I'm gonna say I tried to stop you but you went crazy and forced me with your creepy mind powers."

"That's okay, I'll turn states evidence and sing like a bird. I have a wonderful singing voice."

I laugh, "I bet you do. Thank you, Kate." I don't look at her, I focus on the readings on the HUD. In case anything happened though, I needed her to know.

"Of course, what are besties for?" I smile and my heart sings. I've never had a friend like her. One who I could always count on no matter what.

The elevator shudders for a second and the odd sense of displacement that comes with quantum relocation passes over us.

"Here we go," I say as the doors open.

The doors open to reveal the exact same scene I had when Luke brought me down here for breakfast. don't know why it's disturbing. I guess my mind insists the doors should have opened in a different location What if another lift had come at the same time? What would happen if two elevators tried to occupy the same space?

"Earth to Arsenal, come in?" Kate says, tapping me on the shoulder as she passes by.

"Right. Epic, which way?"

I am scanning the walls now. The nearest acces point is in the offices used by the staff. Take th hallway off the east side of the restaurant.

Arms up to fire off the IP cannons at a second notice I march forward. Kate draws two slick blac pistols holding them in front of her with her wrists crossed for stability.

"Where'd you learn to use a gun?"

"My dad was big into shooting; he'd even made the Army handgun team. We used to go the range together all the time," she says.

"He sounds cool."

"Sometimes, I think I appreciate him more now than I ever did as a kid. It's hard when you can read everyone's emotions. People often feel one thing and say another. At first it feels like a lie, but as I matured I realized the difference between those two things says more about a person than their words."

A late night restaurant crew walks right in from the service entrance. Two of them freeze but the third turns and high tails it back the way she came.

"Don't do anything stupid," Domino warns them with a wave of her pistol as we walk by. They throw their arms up. I don't see the third and we don't have time to look for her.

Second door on the left. There is increased activity that would suggest the base is on alert.

"The door is locked," she says taking a step back. Epic highlights the frame showing me all the connection points. The door is made of reinforced steel with magnetic locks that fail secure. Cutting the power would just result in a more secure door. That's okay, I can cut other things.

"If we fry it, the clamps will slam shut. Gimmie a sec and we'll do this the old fashion way. Watch our backs."

I reach behind and pull the sword. I could use the particle beam but there's no telling what kind of damage I would do to the system behind it and I need their network intact. Legs spread wide for balance, I swing the blade over my head with both hands. As it hits the apex, Epic triggers the kinetic emitters to increase the weight for more force on the downswing. The blade sparks and screeches its way through the entire left side. I slide it out and heft it up for the next swing.

The pop-pop-pop of Domino's guns fills the hall as I slash through the other side of the door. A swift kick and it flies off the hinges, crashing into the floor with a rolling clang.

"I need two minutes. Here take this." I slam the blade three inches into the floor behind Kate. She's about three times as strong as a normal person so she should be able to wield it no problem.

"I'll keep it handy for close encounters, now go. Times wasting."

I stalk into the office, Epic's wire frame overlay pinpoints exactly where I need to go. This late at night no one is around, thank goodness. I'm doing my very best to not kill. Without any way of knowing who's mind-controlled it would be just too big of a gamble.

The console I need is beeping happily to itself when I rip out the network cable. Lines of code appear on the HUD as Epic hacks their system.

"Regular security... nothing to worry... about so far." Each pause in Kate's speech is punctuated by a grunt or a crunch as she teleports around punching and kicking.

Accessing. This network is connected to the shadow network. Engaging active intrusion protocols.

A roar of automatic fire lights up the hall outside and I take half a step before I remember I can't help her. She rolls through the door, spins, and lays back down on the floor with just her two guns parallel to the ground as she opens fire. Both slides lock back and in one swift motion she ejects the magazines and loads the next ones before locking them forward with a thunk.

"How long? They're sending heavy units, external body armor, that sort of thing."

Thirty seconds to breach... I do not know how long to download Shai-Hulud.

"Another minute, maybe?"

She grins, "You got it." Her form vanishes as she pops out of existence. I hear a scream followed by a string of curses. No gunfire but from the screech of metal I'd say she made use of my sword.

I am in. Shai-Hulud is downloading. I'm sifting the data and... Amelia, you need to see this.

A picture of a boy pops on screen, he couldn't be but seventeen.

This is Harald Ericsson. He fought in WWI. He founded Category-7 just after WWII in the wake of the uproar over the SS use of super-people as weapons of war.

"Right, we know this. It was the outrage to the Nazis use of super-people as weapons that started the registration list."

Another picture pops up, a headline from the New York Times *The Country Morns the Passing*. It shows the funeral for Mr. Ericsson.

"Epic, what's your point? He's been dead since 1950."

I only noticed this because we programmed Shai-Hulud to look for patterns, right? You and I always assumed the CEO of Cat-7 was behind it but we could not ever find any evidence. That is because he is not behind it.

Frustrating, but not unexpected. I mean if I were running an evil corporation I wouldn't be the CEO either, too obvious.

However, a search of their financial statements over the years shows this.

A hundred pay stubs, checking accounts, petty cash withdrawals, deeds, and other paperwork pop on-screen. The very last one is dated fifteen years ago.

"What happened fifteen years ago?"

"Arsenal, it's getting busy out here, we need to go!" Kate yells.

"Crap, how much do we have?"

Enough.

"Have Shai-Hulud dump it all on the Internet. Everything he can before they stop him."

Affirmative.

Domino appears beside me and spins with her back to my chest folding in tight as she can.

"What—"

The walls explode around me and I feel the overpressure even through the suit. The kinetic shields drop to eighty-seven percent. Thankfully, Kate was close enough for them to protect her.

"Time to go," she says as she clamps the sword in place. With a hand on each of my shoulders, she closes her eyes and the world vanishes.

20

W here are we?"
Of all the places she could have taken us, this was the last place I expected. I can't take my eyes off the Eiffel Tower standing tall in the distance. We must be in a high-rise somewhere south of town. I can see the sun moderately high to the East... my body clock isn't ready to go from middle of the night to the next day.

"Don't you have like six degrees? I would think it obvious..."

I shake my head, "I don't have any... and you know what I mean. I'm saying, what is this place?"

Kate unbuckles her holsters, slings, and various knives and tosses them on the brown leather sectional seated comfortably in the sunken living room. I still haven't moved from the spot we appeared at.

"You remember how my powers work? Line of sight teleportation unless I have an empathic link to lock on to, right?"

I nod. "Oh my God, do you have a secret boyfriend?"

She shakes her head and a shadow of a frown crosses her full lips before she slips back into 'happy Kate'. "Not at the moment, no. However, I earned quite a bit of money before I joined the Diamondbacks and since... well, the pay isn't bad and like I said, the toy line keeps me flush. I maintain this as my *home away from home.*" She looks around the modest apartment with its leather furniture and paintings on the wall.

It hits me... Kate has a life. Other than being Domino and the teams PR manager. She has a life, she does things. Things like this. Things I've denied myself during my crusade. A hollow pit forms in my stomach and I badly want the armor off.

Amelia, I am detecting abnormal readings on your vitals... are you okay?

"Yes—no... I don't know." I stumble over to the couch, hoping it is sturdy enough to take me and I sink into it. I'd kill for a Coke right about now. I don't think I've ever been this exhausted in my life.

Kate slips out of the room for a moment and I use her absence to think. I can't worry about might-have-been. There is only the here-and-now. Focus Amelia!

Right. Cat-7 as a front. The Cabal. Mind control conspiracy. End of the world. Sobering thoughts indeed.

Kate comes back in cradling the largest, fattest cat I have ever seen. Not that I've seen a lot of them. She has short blue fur and a fluffy tail that swishes back and forth as she rubs between her ears.

"This is Tigress. Until I met you she was my best friend, weren't you girl?" She rubs her face into the cat's neck while she speaks.

"Your powers work on animals?"

"One-way they do. I can read her emotions but since I mostly use pheromones and contact chemicals to alter people's states, nothing I can do makes her happy or sad. She just loves me like I love her."

"Kate, you're the most popular person I know. If we were in high school you'd be the prom queen. How am I your only friend?"

She smiles and not for the first time I see sorrow behind her eyes.

"Amelia, for a smart person you can be pretty dense."

So I keep telling myself. Quantum physics is easier than figuring out people. Kate has everything I've heard of people wanting. Great body, admiration, I don't think I've ever heard anyone say anything bad about her or her alter ego. She's smart, sexy, I could go on. I'm just happy to be her friend and...

"Bingo," she says doing that thing where she answers my emotions and not my words.

"Wait, I still don't get it."

"How many guy friends do you think I have?"

"Tons, I imagine," I say.

She shakes her head as she puts down Tigress who proceeds to wraps herself around Kate's legs and purr like a cell phone on vibrate.

"Other than Luke and Pierre? None. Tommy is nice and I hope he and I can be friends but he has to acclimate to my pheromones first... until then I try to keep my distance. Any other guy I might want to be friends with I have to be very careful." She flops down on the couch next to me with a sigh. "Even if I didn't have powers, guys always take any sign of interest as sexual interest. That's just the way they're wired. Of course, there are always exceptions. For instance, the way you and Carlos are."

I nod, "But I'm safe, right? He knows we can't have a relationship because of... things... so it is safe to be friends with me."

She smiles, "Yep. I'm never safe, I'm always 'available'," she puts air quotes over it. "Then there's the girls. I irritate the hell out of most women. Either from my pheromones or because whenever I'm with a group of people I'm always the center of attention. I can't hang out with anyone who's married." She shakes her head, half-smiling half-sighing as she rubs her eyes. "I had a good friend once. She got married and I was her bridesmaid. This was... six years ago? I'd been out of the Academy for two years and working for the..." she looks alarmed for a moment and then shakes her head, "I guess it doesn't matter now. I worked for the CIA after brain school but before the Diamondbacks."

"Wow, cool. I had no idea."

"It was a secret. Doesn't really matter now that we're wanted fugitives. Anyway, I'm at this wedding and I had a little too much to drink and every guy there is hitting on me... including her brand new husband."

She falls back on the couch rubbing her hands down her face with a long sigh.

"That was the last time I had a friend I could just hang out with and talk too until you came along."

I trigger the faceplate so she can see my face, "What makes me so special?"

"I have no idea. You're not jealous of me, you don't begrudge me, you just accept me. I guess that makes you an awesome person."

"Maybe, but I'm an awesome person in a suit of armor since we left for New York and it's getting ripe in here."

"Can you take it off?"

"Not without my lab or my mobile. But that's roaming the streets of Phoenix."

A tone beeps letting me know Epic has something for me. Kate has a huge TV in one corner and it has the 'smart TV' logo. Epic wirelessly connects displaying his words for us both.

I have finished my analysis of the data and I think I have discovered what is going on. Though, you might find it improbable to believe.

I glance at Kate, who is wearing the same expression as me. After the last twenty-four hours, that seems unlikely. A vast array of images pops up on the screen. Nine men, each in their late twenties, early thirties. From black and white photos that are obviously old to color, pre-digital camera images. All the photos line up on the left side and the financial statements show one by one on the right.

What do you see?"

"These men have all worked for Cat-7 since their founding. The first one, Harald Ericsson, the guy in the black and white photo with the military cap, that's him right? The others, I have no idea," Kate shrugs.

This is all data Shai-Hulud gathered while embedded.

"Shai-Hulud?" Kate asks.

"You know, Dune? Tell me you've read Dune..."

"God, Amelia, is everything sci-fi with you?"

"I'm wearing a suit of armor that allows me to fly while talking to my best friend the empath teleporter..."

She concedes, "Fair point. Go on."

Other than Ericsson all of this was scrubbed from public databases. Twelve years ago an advanc virus filtered through every computer in the worl destroying select data... it did so quietly. The data destroyed is about people. Telepaths who attended th academy, mostly. Along with eight of these nine men. There are no public records of them.

"Who are they then?" I ask.

Each one is an F5 telepath who attended the academy before joining Cat-7.

"That's not possible, Epic," Kate says jerking upright as she spoke. Her feet carry her around the room as she slides her finger through long black hair. "You don't just disappear as an F5 anything... let alone a telepath. Who are these men?"

The question is not 'who are these men?' Kate. But, who is this man?

The financial statements unfold lining up next to the pic of the person they're for. Circles highlight their signatures, flashing as Epic compares each one until a composite of all the signatures forms. No matter what letters are used, every name is written by the same hand.

"That would mean he's been around for a hundred years?" she asks, mouth staying open and I can't say mine isn't either.

Probably older since I was able to find a signature in London of one Harald Ericsson arriving to fight in WWI. However, a comparison of a photograph of him before WWI and after founding

Cat-7 shows he is not the same person. Whoever this man is, he is capable of switching hosts, targets telepaths, and has a large team of mind-controlled scientists hiding his existence while he fortifies his hold on the world.

"That's why he wanted the armor. The damn robots."

"How so?" Right, she didn't see them.

"They have these security robots with plasma weapons. They're very advanced but just steel, titanium, carbon fiber, and plastic. All alloys derivative of modern science. Luke, without getting mad, could probably beat one to a pulp."

"But, if they were made of a certain super-genius' armored battle suit though," Kate finishes for me, "They would be nigh indestructible."

"He's making an army capable of defeating whatever supers he can't convert," I say.

And he is killing any telepath that does not join him. I believe Mr. Kana was going to be his next host. Something must have gone wrong and he was forced to kill him.

"Okay, the next question is... what do we do now?" Kate asks. My heart drops. I know who and what we're up against, but I have no idea how to defeat him.

"First things first, I need to go back to Phoenix and get out of this armor for a while. Can we do that?"

A genuine smile spreads across her lips, "Air Kate is on the job. Let me grab a few things and I'll have you back in the Copper State in no time."

How did you do all of this?" Kate asks as I wheel out of the small RV-like bathroom installed in the back of the semi-rig.

"I didn't, Epic did."

"He doesn't have any hands."

Laughing, I wheel over to the mini fridge and pop the tab on a Coke. The cold soda feels good going down. It doesn't hurt that I've had eight hours sleep and a solid meal.

"You'd be amazed what you can order over the Internet."

It's been sixteen hours since we raided Cat-7 and the news is going crazy. Shai-Hulud dumped virtually everything about them. Including a memo to make sure state teams were mishandled to allow for organic disasters to happen. I couldn't believe it when I saw it in writing. The way Cat-7 treated the Diamondbacks in the past totally makes sense now. Luke is going to be so relieved. I thought it was just Arizona, but it's *everyone.* The more the state teams screwed up the more Cat-7 would hire lobbyist and grassroots movements to put more of the teams in direct control of the big company by saying 'the States can't handle the responsibility'. I'm guessing Ericsson, or whatever name he goes by now, hoped to bring them all under his influence for his takeover bid. Well, that's going up in flames now.

The TV switches to a live broadcast of the FBI and DMHA agents raiding their New York corporate HQ. Not just any agents either, ones with superpowers. If they try anything... I guess Ericsson doesn't have as much pull in the government as I thought he did. Or at least not openly.

"Wow, talk about history in the making. Cat-7 founded the state militias. They're the whole reason the super teams are organized and now," Kate snaps her fingers, "they're gone."

"Ask yourself this: are we better off because of them? Or have they been holding back the super teams since the beginning?"

"Good point."

"This is all great and all, but it still brings us no closer to Ericsson. If he's the telepath who altered my parents then he's the only one who can undo it."

"I know you want that, but there is the possibility it can't be undone, you know this, right?" Kate asks.

I shake my head and wave the thought away, "I'm not ready to accept it as a possibility, not yet. Otherwise, what's the point of continuing? No, I need to find him, Kate. I was hoping something in all these records would point to him but so far, no such luck."

Epic scoured both Cat-7's servers and the Cabals and nothing gave us a central location or secret HQ. I opened up the files on my tablet and started browsing, glancing really, hoping my subconscious would trigger on something. The TV flashes through a few different stories, the raid on the underground bases, the Department of Corrections arresting everyone in the UltraMax while cheering inmates watch. On live TV the President orders the Brigade to turn themselves in at ADX Florence in Colorado. The military equivalent to North Dakota's UltraMax. Not surprisingly, Behemoth and Mariposa have disappeared. How many are in it because they're mind-controlled and how many because they are with this guy? At first I thought everyone would have to be mind-controlled but clearly, people are evil.

"Do you think they can clear our names now?" Kate asks as we watch.

"Can you contact the Arizona AG and find out?"

"I have a few channels. It might take me a day or so. I'd have to go in person..."

"Kate, you need your life back. It isn't fair them prosecuting you for what I did."

She shakes her head, "Both of us or no deal. Besides, that can wait until we figure out what to do next."

"Epic, when we were fighting the Brigade, you recorded everything on Artemis, right?"

Who exactly do you think I am?

"Right," I chuckle, "Can you replay and give me the energy signatures and magneto scans if we have them?"

An idea forms, a glimmer of a plan really. It hinges on if he recorded the right info...

When we were fighting it really felt like the battle took forever but to see it now... it lasted less than three minutes.

"Damn," Kate says under her breath when Behemoth slaps her hands together, "I'm both sorry I missed it and not sorry."

"I'm just glad everyone's okay. Luke heals fast and Pierre was able to put himself in some kind of magic coma to enhance his healing. No one died, it's a win," I say as I watch the sky light up from the impact of the Arrow.

"You put a weapon in space... isn't that illegal?"

"I'm not a country, I can do whatever I like in space. Epic, play back the last part from my armor and from orbit, scans side by side please and half speed."

He does.

"What are you looking for?"

"Remember the thing about Tesla waves?"

Just as the Arrow hits Behemoth's magnetic signature goes off the charts. As if her powers are responding to the threat by amping up.

"Yeah?"

"I think I can find Behemoth using them. If she's with Mariposa and they are with Ericsson..."

"Then we're in business!"

"Yes we are. Epic, task Artemis to look for her magnetic signature. Now that we know what to look for we should be able to find her. I don't think it would work with any other super. She's just incredibly powerful so her magnetic field is commensurate."

Reconfiguring... scanning. Oh no.

"That isn't good," I say.

I'm detecting her magnetic signature, as well as the power source of over ten-thousand of their security bots, in a warehouse located a half mile from the White House.

"The White House?" Kate asks. I hear the incredulity in her voice. If they're in DC...

"Epic, locate every world leader with super-powered assets along with-"

There is a conference in DC hosted by the United States. I believe Luke was there with the governor. Over thirty heads of state are in various cities on the east coast. Now that I know what to look for I am picking up over a hundred-thousand security bots. I am reclassifying them as 'warbots'. Amelia, I think—

"I know," I say. I can't believe it, but I know.

"Know what?"

"The only reason he would want the armor would be to make the warbots unstoppable. The only reason for that would be he plans a coup de'tat... against the world and it's happening right now."

"But he didn't get it which means..."

"Arsenal is the only unstoppable armor. Let's hope we're in time and it's enough. I need to suit up. We need to get the word out. Epic?"

Standing by.

"Alert every team, every government agency, tap into the EBS if you have to. Initiate 'Firefly' protocol."

Confirmation of Firefly protocol required.

"Confirmed."

"Okay all the Star Wars and Star Trek references I get, but what about Firefly fits here?"

"You can't stop the signal, Kate. Epic always operates from the position of staying invisible. I just authorized him to get the word out no matter what." She rolls her eyes as I wheel into position.

"Amelia, maybe you should call your parents..."

I shake my head. They don't remember me anyways and I can't afford to let those emotions in right now.

"I can't, Kate. Not right now. I need you to get to the Arizona AG and try and make him understand what is about to happen. He won't believe you... Hell, I can barely believe it, but you have to try."

"On it. Good luck." She reaches out and squeezes my shoulder. I snake a hand up and put it on hers and hold her there for a moment.

"Thank you for being my friend."
She smiles and vanishes.
"Epic... initiate!"

E ven at our top speed of Mach 4 it will still take too
long, a whole forty-two minutes...
"Epic, we don't have that kind of time. How's the
warning going?"

*I have almost cracked the EBS network. I
hacked homeland and put them on 'high alert'.
However, it is difficult to give them an exact threat to
defend against. They are already on alert because of
the visiting dignitaries. Amelia, even if every agent
turns out to be on our side, the probability of success
is low. Even a 'best outcome' is likely to result in
significant civilian casualties and fatalities among
foreign dignitaries.*

"I think we need to go sub-orbital on this. Do the
math, I feel the need for speed." The Emdrive kicks in

full power and Phoenix shrinks followed by Arizona. The sky above dims and the stars come out as the altimeter passes eighty-thousand feet. Epic puts a path on the HUD showing me where to go and how fast. The altimeter switches from feet to miles as we blow past sixteen.

We have now exceeded the SR-71's flight record.

While the top speed in the atmo is limited by how much heat builds up around the suit after I break the sound barrier, I won't have that limitation when I slip the atmospheric bounds.

At thirty miles the atmo starts thinning and my speed shoots up. The HUD automatically switches from MPH to Miles Per Second. I let out a whoop. Four-point-nine miles per second and we hit a hundred miles up in less than two minutes.

I take a deep breath. The Earth is beautiful from up here. The icy black of space above and the blue gem below. I could seriously get used to this. The HUD shows me DC's local time. Just after five pm. Hard to believe that only twenty-four hours has passed since I came back from New York. At least I caught some sleep and food.

Congratulations, Amelia. You are the first person to achieve astronaut status without the aid of a shuttle or superpowers.

I've always wanted to do this. I just wish I could spend a few minutes enjoying it.

"Epic, have the truck start heading east, you never know if we'll need it when this is done."

Roger. Do you have plans on how to deal with Behemoth?"

"No," I sigh, "Not without killing her. I suppose I'm justified at this point but... I don't like it."

I am glad you do not. You would not be the little girl who created me if you did.

It's suddenly very tight in the armor. Epic is my friend, he's my family. I've had him almost as long as I've been on my own.

"Epic, whatever happens tonight I want... need... two things from you."

Go ahead.

"I want you to know how important you are to me. Thank you, for everything."

Of course. You are my creator and my friend.

"Second, you survive. If something happens and the armor is—breached... you survive. Understood?"

Understood.

216

"Okay, let's go be heroes."

The drive goes full power and I shoot through space at a crazy velocity without atmospheric drag. My eyes bug when we hit ten miles per second. Damn, if I had the capacity to load more air and maybe some food we could make a trip to the moon.

"Epic make a note, let's look at setting foot on the moon!"

Note made. Even I would think that was awesome.

"I know right?" I can't help but shout for joy as we burn through the upper atmosphere. My faceplate optics polarize as heat build-up creates a light too bright for human eyes.

We are going to perform a flip... hold on to your lunch.

"Oh boy," I manage to gurgle as we execute the maneuver. I pull my knees up as he cuts the thrust and I roll forward. Once I'm falling feet first I extend them again—slowly—and he locks the suit up and fires thrusters.

We are unable to communicate with the ground for the next two minutes. When we emerge we will be dead center over DC.

"Roger that."

The countdown pops up on the HUD and I start sweating. Not because of the heat, but because what is about to happen. Ericsson jump-started his plans because of me. Logically I know he's off balance. He's reacting, not acting. Which means he wasn't fully ready to move on the government.

Still... thousands of warbots. Who knows what heroes and villains they have on their side and even then... I still have to go into this with the intent to kill Behemoth.

It is war, Amelia.

"You a mind reader now?"

No. But I am thinking it too. Communications blackout passes in five...four...three...

The optics depolarize, allowing me to see again. We're a hundred thousand feet up and everything seems so small.

Amelia, brace for—

The sky lights up and for a heartbeat my optics stay open nearly blinding me before going dark again.

"What was that?"

Non-nuclear electromagnetic pulse weapon. If we were not shielded against a nuclear EMP we would be falling dead. However, I have lost comms with everyone. The greater DC area is devoid of power.

He isn't exaggerating. There's a massive black hole looming below us where a city full of lights stood a few seconds before. No traffic, no buildings, no beacons.

"Any aircraft in the area?"

Thankfully all aircraft have been diverted for security reasons.

A flash of light catches my eye. I can see it now that we're only a few thousand feet up. Thousands of camouflaged warbots marching through the city. Occasional bursts of green light flare through the night as they open up with their plasma weapons.

The majority of the fire is happening at the Capitol building and the White House.

"Unlock," I order. Arms forward, we shoot off toward Pennsylvania Ave. Congress may or may not be in session, but there are lots of congress members. There's only one president and while I may not have voted for him... he's the symbol of our country. If Ericsson manages to kill him then it will be that much harder to stop his evil plans.

"Go full ECM, give me a scan of the area. Bring up Artemis and have her for backup. Once comms are re-established try and coordinate this mess as best you can. Break whatever laws you have too."

Understood. I have located Behemoth. She is engaged US Marshals and Secret Service meta-human teams at the white house.

"I see it." I don't normally curse but I want to right now. It's a frigging disaster. Part of the White House is burning. Overturned armored fighting vehicles and a hundred bodies litter the lawn.

"Full power to everything, unlock the safeties on the Particle Beams and go auto on the grenade launcher." The HUD flashes as it switches to angry red. Weapons status, shields, and power levels all become easier to read.

I'm not set up to fight a war. Fifteen grenades against thousands of warbots isn't even a contest, more like a slaughter—mine.

They spot me at a few hundred feet. Fifty mechanical heads turn at once raising their weapons to fire.

I cut power to the boots and fall right at them. I hear the *puff-puff-puff* of the grenade launcher lighting up targets. No pods or bean bags today, nothing but HE. The explosions rip through their metallic hides, setting off a series of secondaries as whatever powers them reacts badly to the explosions.

I hit the ground a hundred feet from where Behemoth is pounding the tar out of a woman I don't know. The US Marshal I met a while back, Bricklayer, ineffectively punches Behemoth from behind trying to force her to release the agent. There is a volume of small and medium arms fire as pistols, smgs, and heavy machine guns fire from every window pouring down lead on the army of warbots. I can only thank God and Epic that Ericsson never figured out how to replicate my armor.

"Particle beams, sustained fire!"

Arms straight out from my shoulders, wrist down, they fire. Hyper-accelerated silicon spews out at near light speed. Epic shows me where to aim as I rush forward, decapitating and decimating everything the beams touch. Metal slags as the beams pass through countless warbots.

The world lights up and I'm upside down, flying through the air. My teeth rattle when I hit the cratered concrete walkway just outside the White House.

Close proximity plasma detonation. Amelia, get up!

Right! I roll over and kick in the jets. Two warbots come from behind the flipped over AFV and I tear right through them.

"How's Bricklayer?"

He is incapable of slowing her down.

I risk a glance at the field and I cringe. My stomach threatens me but I bear down on it. The poor woman is dead. Her body beaten to an unrecognizable pulp. As I watch, Behemoth puts Bricklayer through an armored vehicle. I don't know if he's getting back up.

We need to engage her. She is the single most powerful super in America, possibly the world. Amelia, I know you did not want to set out to kill her, but I have run the numbers. The only way to stop her is to kill her.

He's right. I've killed before but only accidentally. "Unlock the sword." The blade clicks free as I pull it around. The particle beams might pierce her hide but they would take time. She survived an orbital strike not twenty-four hours ago. No, it's this or nothing. I swing a few times to loosen up my arm. I can't imagine this is going to be easy.

"Epic, we'll need maximum weight when I swing."

Roger.

I run at her. There are moments I wish I could feel what it is like to run, to flex my toes in the carpet, to really move my legs and not just have actuators moving them for me while responding to my nervous system. Maybe one day, not today.

I raise the sword up over my head and leap into the air. The Emdrive kicks in adding extra oomph.

Behemoth has Bricklayer's neck in one massive hand. She's holding him up like he's made of paper. His face is a mass of bruises and blood. She tosses him aside and spins around to face me a half second before I bring the blade down on her.

God forgive me.

The sword hits her forearm and I slam into the ground—the blade bites a half inch into flesh and comes to a halt against bone. She screams, whipping her arm aside, dragging me with her since my hands are kinetically locked to the sword. The blade tears free from her flesh and I tumble end over end through the side lawn to come to rest against a wall.

It did not work.

"You think?" Oh, man, she's pissed. Blood flows freely down her arm. Epic had to let the sword go while we tumbled so it didn't cut me. I search for it and try to stand at the same time. The ground shakes as she stomps her way toward me.

No time for the sword, I flip my arms up, wrist down and fire both Particle Beams. Light flashes as they burn through the air to her. She screams as the silicon particles smash into her, instantly burning through her costume but splashing off her skin.

"I can't believe your stupid sword cut me!" She hurls a chunk of concrete through the air. I shift the beams to shatter it into a million pieces. She plows through the dust and slams one giant fist against me.

Amelia...

"Five more minutes," I mutter. Then the pain hits and I sputter to life coughing up blood on my HUD.

Move!

Everything hurts, I have no idea where I am but I can't argue with his advice. I trigger the jets and I'm up in the air a half second before an AFV crashes into the ground where I was a moment before. She knocked me through a corner of the building and I only came to rest against a concrete pillar.

"Epic, I don't know what to do. I can avoid dying by keeping her at a distance but I can't stop her. The second she figures this out she's going to resume her mission."

Down!

I cut the jets as two plasma balls explode above me.

"Comms back yet?"

For us. Not for anyone else.

"I should have made Artemis an actual comsat." I hit the ground, staggering a few feet before I regain my balance. My chest is on fire and it hurts to breathe. Everything hurts.

Amelia, you require medical attention.

"Where is she?"

She just ripped the door off the White House and is proceeding to the elevator leading to the underground bunker. She figured it out fast.

If I recall right that bunker can take a near direct hit from a nuke.

"Epic broadcast what you can from Artemis. I know she's not commercially connected but figure something out! We need backup."

What are you going to do?

"Improvise."

It only takes a second to get back around the front. The devastation is incomprehensible. Behemoth simply ignores everything and everyone as she pounds her way through reinforced steel security doors. I land at the entrance and follow her in.

Two agents in black coats with shotguns turn on me and I raise my hands, "One of the good guys."

"The fact that you aren't killing us already makes me believe you. Can you stop her?" He points to Behemoth.

"I'm not sure. You guys should run, she's about to come this way in a hurry." They scatter and I'm glad. I'd come to terms with killing her when I thought I could. Now, I'm desperately trying to figure out a way to do it. The sword should have lopped off her arm. Nothing is that indestructible, not against a one molecule thick blade. It should've worked.

Arms forward, wrist down, I light off the particle beams. They strike her dead center in the back. I can see smoke rising as her outfit vaporizes followed by her skin blackening. She turns, snarling at me through a mask of rage.

"You? I am going to peel you out of that tin can and bathe in your blood!"

Warning lights on my HUD tell me the particle beams are in danger of over-heating.

"You're going to have catch me first," I fire up the jets and fly backward trying to keep the beams on her as I move. She *leaps* at me. I don't have time to react and a distant part of my brain wonders why I didn't think this was a possibility? She crashes into me, her massive weight overrides the jets and we slam against the concrete outside. Using her knees she pins me to the ground. I didn't even see her move, not really.

"What was that about catching you?" She laughs as she reaches down to grab my helmet.

A bolt of lightning arcs through the air to light the night in a single frozen moment. She glances up and I do too as a familiar spear falls through the air at impossible speed slamming into the ground point first.

Protector lands in a thump, the shockwave of his arrival splashes debris in every direction. The spear leaps to his hand and he holds it out to her, point first. He's every bit as impressive as the first time I saw him.

"Surrender, Karen, I won't ask a second time."

"Your parlor tricks might scare the newbs, *Sydney,* but I ain't afraid of you." She slams my head into the ground to make a point before standing and stomping on my chest.

I roll out of the way, coughing painfully as I do so.

"Epic, did you get a signal out?"

Negative, I have not successfully restored communications.

Pythia, then. I guess she decided to side with me over her visions.

Based on their level of strength I suggest you move before they collide.

"Good point," I say, launching into the air. A list of systems flash yellow and crimson with damage. IP Cannons are offline, I'm down to one Particle Beam, no grenades, and no sword. There are still thousands of warbots to deal with. I'd EMP them but clearly, they're shielded.

A crack like thunder explodes bellow me and a massive shockwave blasts through the air. Behemoth halls herself back and slams into his shield again. Protector actually slides backward from the blow. The ground around their feet pulverizes as do the nearest vehicles.

"Epic? He can take her, right?"

I do not have enough data to predict the outcome reliably. There are other things we could do. Other leaders who need our help.

"I know, but Sydney is here because of me. All of this is because of me. Maybe what Pythia saw was me forcing Ericsson's hand and thus ending in annihilation."

Possibly.

"My point is—he's here because of me and if he loses then it's my fault. We've got to help him!"

How? All of our weapons have been ineffective. Even a direct hit from an Arrow is unlikely to even render her unconscious.

I fire off my one working particle beam into the melee of swirling fists and spears. I nail her shoulder with no visible effect. I'm not even sure she feels it. "Set the beam to pulse, at least that way I can use it longer."

Too bad I can't get her to swallow a ZPFM. Her fist clangs off Protector's shield and he swipes at her with his spear. The point slashes her skin and I see blood dripping off the bronze tip.

"Epic! The spear can hurt her."

So could your sword, but not enough.

Her hand flashes out at a chunk of rubble and she hurls it at me. At the same time Protector shield checks her to the ground. I dodge the concrete and Rebar projectile and land a few yards from them, my one working particle beam pointing at her.

"Give up, Karen, your cause is lost. Once we locate your master, he will be too." Protector has her pinned with his spear hovering over her abdomen.

This is better than I hoped for. If he can force her surrender then we can find out—

She grabs the spear and yanks it toward her. The point penetrates her stomach but the motion forces Protector off balance and he falls toward her. Faster than I can shout a warning she slams her hands together over his ears with the force of a thunderclap.

Sydney, The Protector, the one hero I admired growing up, stumbles off of her barely keeping his feet as he sways from side to side before falling to his knees then face first against the ground. He takes one last breath... then his heart stops.

My vision dims and I can hardly breathe. All I can hear is my heart pounding.

Blood pours from his ears, pooling on the ground around his face. Behemoth laughs as she stands. The spear's tip still wedged in her side. She yanks at it but the arrow-shaped weapon is wedged into her ribs and she roars in rage when it won't dislodge.

"You're next," she growls, holding the still embed spear up, she charges. In shock, I don't react quick enough and she hits me—hard.

The HUD scrambles as the armor impacts the ground. Alarms scream at me as the kilo-pascals rise beyond tolerance. The ZPFM output highlights as it shoots through the roof dumping power into the kinetic shields just to keep me alive.

I can see Sydney, lying face down in his own blood. He was so nice and selfless. He didn't deserve to die. Not the man who took me into space for the first time. Not the man who gave people, gave me, hope.

Over the alarms, I scream at Behemoth. I don't think she can hear me, I'm not even sure my PA is working. I reach for the spear, trying to grab it as she jerks around sending the short shaft flying wildly. It's inside her a good six inches at least.

"Your armor is tough but you can't take this forever." She lifts her foot up to curb stomp me and I manage to find a handful of haft.

"Behemoth, I may not be able to kill you, but you can't fly."

She pauses, looking down at me then to the haft in my hand.

In my mind, with all my will I scream—*Take me to the moon.*

With as much strength as I have left I shove the spear forward. Whether it's Pythia or the grace of God, the spear takes over from there. Behemoth screams as the magical weapon leaps up to the sky, carrying her with it faster than I can track. In the blink of an eye, she's gone. I don't know if she needs to breathe or not, but I sure as hell hope she does.

I fall back to the ground. I'm done. All I can see is poor Sydney as the world turns black.

*A*melia, *wake up. Communications have been restored and reinforcements are inbound.*

"Wake up?" my voice slurs and my mouth feels like cotton candy. The sky is still dark. Sort of. I can't see out of the right side of my faceplate.

"Epic, why can't I see?"

Some of the optical sensors in the suit have sustained damage. They will need to be replaced.

"Fantastic," I mutter. Everything hurts. A groan escapes as I roll over.

The Protector. I can't believe she killed him. He's still there, kneeling face down almost as if he were praying, but he isn't. His words come back to me, he said if he were ever to die, she would find a new one. That's a cold comfort for the man who gave his life to help me.

"Amelia?"

Luke's deep voice and the concern that one word carries is sweet relief to my pain wracked body.

"Luke? Where are you?" The air pops and he's next to me, his big hands helping me up. There's a rapid series of pops as Kate brings the whole team with the exception of Pierre.

"Mr. Perfect is still in his magically induced coma," Luke says.

"Were you able to get through to the Arizona AG?" I ask Kate. Epic is running through a checklist of damaged components while we talk and I try not to be distracted by the laundry list of repairs needed. He's bypassing what he can but it isn't pretty.

I need some form of self-repair. Nanites maybe? But how could I have them repair the exoskeleton? Maybe some form of temporary—

"...the bottom line is he believes us, but with the mass attack there isn't a lot he can do."

I shake my head to focus. I missed what she said but I caught the gist of it.

"Fleet, inside the White House, are a couple of agents, make sure the President is secure and let them know Behemoth is gone," I tell the speedster.

"On it." He vanishes in an eddy of dust.

"Glacier," she turns to me and I can see some micro-fractures in her ice from the fires nearby. Thank goodness Luke leaped in front of her. "These warbots are using plasma weapons. High energy gas super accelerated until it is a few thousand degrees. I want you and Tommy—"

He re-appears in a blur. "They say the President is secure. Without the threat of Behemoth, they're confident they can take it from here."

"Great. Fleet, take Glacier and you two are on fire duty. These weapons are a menace and with the rampaging warbots and other supers those fires are going to quickly get out of control."

"Arsenal, you're bleeding," Glacier says pointing at my waist. I look down as best I can, not easy to do in the armor. My hand comes away bloody but I realize it isn't mine. It's hers.

"Not mine, but thanks, get on it."

She nods. Tommy picks her up and disappears in a blur.

"What about us?" Kate asks.

"Somewhere out here there are more supers on Ericsson's side. Epic is compiling a list based on the data that we have. There are several spots that need help. Mostly FBI and Homeland agents who aren't powered trying to protect people from super-powered assets. We're going to be their backup."

"Sounds good. Amelia, Kate filled me in on what's going on with Ericsson. I know why you didn't share and I want you to know I understand." He puts his arms around me and pulls me close. Even though I can't feel him through the suit I sink into his hug.

"You do? I was so worried..." All my emotions bubble up and my vision blurs worse than it already was. I can't cry! No way to wipe my face but damn if I didn't need to hear this.

"I'm a Marine, silly, tactics and operational security I understand."

I hold on to him a few more seconds then I can let go. We part hesitantly, oh how do I wish I could take the armor off.

I have taken over dispatching pretty much every emergency service on the Eastern Seaboard. With the main lines down I have tasked Artemis to scan for the hot spots. I have also hacked NSA's Keyhole and have three of them relaying info to emergency responders. 911 dispatchers from across the country are coming online as I send the signals to them and use the satellites to guide first responders. Their first priority is the civilians.

"Wow, well done. I guess there is no putting the genie back in the bottle after this?"

Unlikely. Perhaps having saved the President from a gruesome death will be enough to earn you a pardon?

"Let's hope. Where we going?"

The Prime Minister of England is in Baltimore and is under the biggest threat. We can be there in two minutes.

"Okay, here is the plan—"

24

Forty-eight hours later and my bruises have bruises Between Epic's early warning and our timely intervention, we managed to save every world leader and keep the civilian casualties to a minimum. If this was Ericsson's big push, then he failed miserably. The word is out, not just on him, but every super, hero or villain, that sided with him or was mind-controlled by him.

The only loose end is I still have no idea where he is or how to find him and even if I did, I don't know if I could convince him to undo the damage he did to my parents.

The good news is, in the two solid days of fighting and rescuing, my truck arrived. Currently, I'm resting on the couch drinking a Coke while watching Epic's automated machinery do the repairs on my suit.

We're parked outside the hotel where the team is sleeping. The city is still working on restoring power to the area so I opted to stay in the rig where I have electricity and all the TV I could want.

The HD cam on the back shows Luke about to knock on the door when Epic triggers it open.

"You can't sneak up on an AI," I yell around the corner. The couch is in the front just behind the lab and the door is all the way in the back.

"I wasn't trying to sneak up. I just thought you would like some pizza."

"Oh boy, do I!" I don't think I've ever been so excited to eat. The smell of pepperoni and cheese sets my stomach growling. I'd run over to him and wolf it down if I could. I excitedly pat the seat next to me, "Come on!"

He leaps in the truck with one smooth motion and trots over. "I'd like to think you'd be this happy to see me even if I didn't bring the pizza."

I open the box, it isn't Bianco's but even bad pizza is good pizza.

"My Dad always said, 'don't ask questions you don't want the answer to'."

"Sounds like a smart man, I can't wait to meet him."

I swallow the first bite of cheesy goodness and let my body fully understand that it now has access to food.

"Well," I say around a second mouthful, "You might. I don't know. I just... They still have no idea they even have a daughter. How am I supposed to deal with that? There are two people, they look, talk, act exactly like I remember my parents. They just have no idea who I am. What do I do?"

He slides in next to me, carefully lifting my legs to rest on his lap. "I wish I could tell you, really. You're very smart though, if you haven't noticed, I think you'll do fine."

I stick my tongue out at him, "You're no help at all."

"I'm willing to listen if you want to bounce ideas off my thick skull."

"Other than finding Ericsson and making him undo what he's done? I have no idea."

"Amelia, the whole world knows who was behind this, everyone is looking for him. I'm sure he will turn up."

It was true, Epic provided every law enforcement agency on the planet with all the evidence we had on exactly what Ericsson had done. How he could change bodies and fool telepaths was still a big question.

Luke absently massages my foot while he speaks, "It's too bad the warbots didn't have some kind of signal you could hack- what?"

I'm an idiot. "Epic!"

Processing.

"During the fight, the warbots responded to our actions. Not just in self-defense but they had tactics and initiative. I thought they were just well programmed, but what if they did have a signal, hidden in the noise where no one would hear it?"

"Wouldn't it have been destroyed when the EMP went off?"

I shake my head and throw back the rest of the Coke, "Nope. They're shielded. All the EMP would do is remove all the noise."

"How does that help us now?"

It helps us because during the fight I used Artemis to record every signal as well as act as a communications hub. An examination of the logs shows radio waves at one-hundred and forty-five megahertz.

"Where did they come from?"

The signal originated... in orbit.

"So he has a satellite like me? And why does that freq sound familiar?"

It is the frequency NASA uses to speak to the ISS Hub.

"Could he be using the space station as a relay?"

I glance at poor Luke, his eyes have glazed over. He quietly eats a slice of pizza waiting for me to make my 'aha' sound. I don't know if I can. If he's using the Space Station as a relay he could be anywhere on Earth.

I do not think so. I am not seeing any other transmissions. It would be safe to assume that if he were planning something then he would assume victory. At which point no one would be left to challenge him.

"Are you saying he's *on the space station?*"

Affirmative.

Luke clears his throat to get my attention, "How can you know he's up there?"

"Epic? What do you know?"

More than I have time to recount?

"That is what I get for programming you with a sense of humor. I mean, how do we prove he's up there?"

I am not sure we can. But it would not hurt to go up and take a look, would it?

"No, it wouldn't."

"Go up? Into space? You can do that?"

Luke looks genuinely shocked and a little awed.

"Can and have."

"I don't suppose you can take me with you?" he asks.

"Sadly, no, but I can't go until the repairs are complete which means we can spend the night here..."

"I..." He pauses as understanding dawns on him and his face turns an adorable shade of red.

"Come over here and kiss me," I tell him.

He does.

Amelia, we need a full lab and a few more weeks to have the armor at one-hundred percent. I do not recommend this course of action.

"I know, but I want my parents back, Epic. We know where he is *right* now. If he comes back to Earth I may never find him."

I hate arguing with a computer. They're almost always right. However, I have to do this and do it right frigging now. The readout on the monitor tells me all the reasons I shouldn't. The left particle beam is still offline, the optics on the right aren't repaired, I'll need to fabricate a new helmet, and my grenade launcher is offline. This leaves me with propulsion, sensors, life support, and about thirty-percent of my weapons including my sword. I had the scare of my life until I found it buried under a half vaporized AFV.

"Right now he's off-balance, his plans for who knows how long have come undone. If we strike we have the upper hand."

I am with you, as always. I just do not advise it.

"And that is why we're not telling anyone because they wouldn't advise it either. But this is about my parents, Epic, if there's even a small chance I can make this work then we have to take it."

Understood.

That's something, I guess. I wheel over to the spot marked on the floor. The pull bar comes down to lift me out of my chair. With all the damage to the suit I couldn't put it back in the chair configuration, leaving me with the old-fashioned way.

"Epic, initiate!"

Ten minutes later we are soaring straight up past the first three sound barriers. I wish this were more exhilarating. Instead, all I feel is a hollow pit in my stomach. I really hope I'm not making a mistake here.

The higher we go the faster I can accelerate until I'm hitting five miles per second and we're out of the atmosphere entirely. Life support chugs away at eighty percent power in a losing battle to keep me warm as the cold of space wraps around us.

Orbit.

When Sydney brought me up here I didn't have time to look around, nor when I went sub-orbital to get to DC. Now, I have some extra time. I just wish the right side of my vision wasn't blurry.

"Okay, enough sightseeing, where's the station?"

Displaying course now.

A yellow line appears on my HUD. It's weird, I usually have landmarks to navigate as a frame of reference. Up here it is just the black on one side and blue on the other. The only way I know I'm going in the right direction is the three-dimensional path Epic displays on the HUD. If I stay in the center I am in the pipe and going the right way.

The thrusters hum as they push me through the frictionless environment. Electromagnetic propulsion was made for outer space. I have to dump gigawatts of extra power from the ZPFM to make it work right in atmo, but up here? I could probably hit a few thousand miles per second without much effort. Of course, the second a solar flare hits or a particle of dust the size of my fingernail crossed my path, I'd be roasted and gutted.

Epic highlights the thousands of objects in orbit to avoid, thankfully NASA tracks all these things making it easy for us. Tapping into their system helps us double check our own onboard sensors and not have to rely on just one mechanism.

"I don't see it yet... you sure this is the right way?"

We are approaching the station from its orbital shadow. Presumably, it will have fewer sensors pointed at where it has been instead of where it is going. However, we are still a hundred miles out, you cannot see it with the naked eye yet.

The seconds tick by as I watch the range shrink. I flip around giving us a retro burst with the boot thrusters slowing us down to just a mile per second.

"Epic, stealth mode, one last burn and let's just pretend we're orbital junk."

Calculating, projecting burn, commence in three, two...

I fire off the Emdrive in the direction he indicates for three seconds. The HUD switches to blue and I go limp, letting our momentum carry us. He locks the armor up with my visor is pointed at the station. Even if they turned radar full power at us, the kinetic field would send it bouncing off in other directions. We have the cross signature of a sparrow in this mode.

"Uh, Epic, we have a problem."

I see it.

I've wanted to say this my whole life, but I never thought I would say it with terror gripping my heart. I swallow a couple of times just to clear the cotton from my mouth.

"That's no space station…"

ISS was a joint venture between several space agencies. Funded mostly by the US, built by space capable supers and shuttle launches. It's a habitat capable of supporting two or three astronauts at most... this ain't that. It might have started life off with as a small habitat, but this is a full-on orbital base capable of housing hundreds.

In the center is an octahedron, like an eight-sided die. Three rings wrap around it crossing each other at different angles almost like a double helix. I can make out light glinting off windows, small vehicles traversing it and two huge landing bays. How the hell did he build this with no one finding out? The whole thing is easily six hundred feet across and at least twelve hundred tall. I can't be sure; it's hard to tell distance in space.

There are elements in the hull I cannot quantify.

"What does that mean?"

Based on light analysis and passive sensors... I have no idea what that thing is made of.

That isn't possible. Like the man said, 'there's nothing new under the sun'. If it exists on Earth then Epic can-

"Epic... holy crap... are you saying what I think you're saying?"

I cannot tell you for certain. Perhaps one of the many scientists he has kidnapped over the years is a metallurgist who created something new. After all, a weightless environment is ideal for forging alloys.

"You say that but I hear the doubt. It's alien isn't it?" The pause before he answers is far too long for comfort.

That would be the most probable likelihood based on all available data.

This is a lot to take in. Aliens. On Earth. It would explain the Zero Point and plasma weapons. Reversed engineered alien tech?

"Epic? What if they had another reason for kidnapping all those top scientists?"

Other than using them for the obvious reasons?

I do the math. Fifteen years ago is when the world's smartest people started disappearing. Almost five years ago all the powerful telepaths vanished. They checked into the school but they never checked out.

"For the last two decades, the worlds technological advances have, essentially, been put on hold, right?"

Begin deceleration bursts, and yes.

I spread my hands out and Epic does microbursts to slow our speed gently as to not catch anyone's attention. Two thousand feet per second... one thousand... five hundred.

The station comes up fast. I know it's an optical illusion but I still close my eyes and tense up.

Impact. I thud against the metal. Epic instantly switches the kinetic field generators to 'stick' me against the hull. I roll over and put my back to the wall. My breath catches in my throat. My God, the world is beautiful from up here.

It takes a second before I regain my train of thought.

"Everyone who could blow the whistle on him has vanished and everyone who could have created an advance to fight him has been usurped. Epic, he's holding our tech level down artificially. Think of all the advances we would've had if he hadn't!"

It is logical to assume the rate of advancement in technology would increase at a statistically average level. I am checking the math now. Adding variables. Creating outcomes. Engaging warp drive.

I smile a big toothy grin. Epic always knows how to put me at ease. While he's running permutations I take a moment to switch the HUD to our passive ECM and see what I can pick up. There is a ton of signal noise. I pick up the camera stream from what everyone thinks is the ISS, not to mention the astronauts as they go through their daily routines. Now I know it's all fabricated.

The station is connected with several satellites and three space telescopes I didn't even know we had.

Compiling the last hundred years of advancements since Tesla turned on Wardenclyffe I have determined that our rate of advancement dropped by almost eight percent over the last fifteen years. It has declined steadily. We did not just hold still. We lost ground.

"Son of a—" I clamp my mouth shut. If I had to guess, he had some kind of program to identify the smartest people capable of making truly great advances. Then he just snatched them up.

"Are we sure it's just fifteen people?"

No. That is all I could find. We could put in a number of variables and estimate up to at least a hundred people. Even if it were just fifteen, that would be enough.

"True. The big leaps are always a single person with a vision, aren't they?"

Edison, Tesla, Wright brothers, Von Braun, Hughes... imagine if they had been removed from the timeline.

"No electricity, at least not then. No planes, no nuclear power, no Rocketeer. Would we have even beaten Hitler?"

It is likely if even one of those men disappeared from the timeline the world would be a very different place. For good or ill is impossible to know. Too many variables.

I've read too many books and played too many games with this kind of premise to doubt it. Maybe we continued at the same rate of advance, but it is unlikely. Before Tesla turned on Wardenclyffe and changed the world forever, few people had heard of him. I can only imagine the world we would live in if he'd been taken well before that time.

"This ends, Epic. Record everything. If you think we're about to die, or if I become mind-controlled, you dump all of this to the world. No matter what happens he can't be allowed to tamper with Earth's future anymore."

Affirmative.

I take one last look at the Pacific Ocean as it passes underneath me. No matter what, I have this moment. I'm in space in a suit I built. No one can ever take that away from me.

"Okay," I take a deep breath, "Let's go kick his ass."

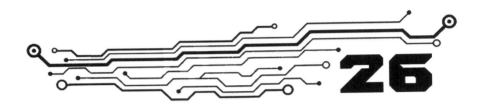

W ith three giant bays on different sides of the
station and numerous hatches, airlocks, and
observation posts, I thought it would be easy to sneal
in.

Nope.

The bays are protected by some kind of pressure
shield that keeps the atmo in and space out. Even
touching them could trigger an alarm. The only other
option is an airlock door or maintenance hatch but the
stupid station doesn't have a wireless network we can
tap to hack them open. Other than the fake one and
that doesn't do us any good.

"We could cut our way in?"

Any hull breach would instantly alert them to our presence.

"They're going to know we're here eventually. I could fire off a couple of Particle Beam from a central location, blow open a couple of holes, pick one at random and go through."

We cannot see the interior. There could be people in the locations you shoot.

I hadn't thought about that. However, I don't think I can get through this without people dying. I won't kill callously, but this has got to stop.

"I think it's worth the chance. Let's do it."

Pushing off the station, I kick in the thrusters. We glide out a few hundred feet. I check the power levels. The ZPFM is undamaged and I have all the power I need for this.

Epic puts the crosshairs on the HUD and I wave them over the station looking for likely spots. There's a hatch, what looks like two observation ports, and a sensor array of some kind.

"Full power, three-second burst. Crap... are we going to be okay heat wise? With no atmo to bleed off the heat..."

Running the numbers. If you fire no more than twenty seconds total we should be okay.

"Alright, let's do this."

I start with the sensor array, wiping out their ability to see might keep them occupied as well as blind.

I place the target over the dishes and antennas sprouting from the hull and bend my wrist down. The particle beam reaches out and touches the array. I let it flash twice before stopping. I can't hear it, but the exhaust of gas and particles are impressive. The dish disintegrates as an entire section fifty feet square explodes outward into space.

"Nice!"

Well done.

The next spot is an observation port, or at least I think it is. I hope no one is in there. The beam lashes out. I draw an 'X' on the window. As the second beam touches the previous burn the entire port explodes outward. Gas, debris, and glass disappear into the black in a heartbeat.

Two thousand degrees on the particle beam emitters.

Crud, okay enough for one more shot. That's okay. I find the hatch, identify the likely weak points... and fire. The beam slices through like butter. Before

I'm done the hatch follows the other two sections into space.

"Okay, time to go."

A fault light pops up on the HUD flashing red before burning a solid crimson.

I am sorry. I thought the emitter could handle the sustained heat.

"Me too. Maybe it suffered damage fighting Behemoth we didn't detect?"

I fly up to the hatch, it's the smallest opening of the three, therefore I'm hoping they'll consider it the least likely entrance. The airlock looks like a maintenance hatch of some kind for drones or small cargo, not people. The ideal entry point as they won't think a person will come through.

There is an internal fail secure airlock door.

I land in the remains of the 'lock and let my boots clamp to the metal deck using my kinetic emitters to approximate gravity.

"That's why I like to keep this handy," I reach behind me and pull the sword from my back, "For close encounters."

You are having fun with this are you not?

"I have no idea what you're talking about," I say with a grin as I slash the square blade down on the control panel. It explodes in a shower of sparks. Next, I start hacking at the door's centerline, I just need to open it enough to crawl through. The blade penetrates the steel and the entire door explodes outward slamming me and flattening the suit against the far wall as air rushes out.

There is another door closing.

"I see it." Ten feet past the one I just destroyed, a massive bulkhead door slides down. I leap forward kicking in the jets and scream through the hatch just before it clamps shut behind me.

There is atmo in here. It is human, normal mix of oxygen, nitrogen, and carbon dioxide.

"Internal network?"

They do have a wireless network inside. The outer shell must be incredibly well shielded. Attempting access...

I glance around; this is a hallway of some kind. Gunmetal gray walls with LED lights every few feet to chase the shadows away. Control panels, caution signs, decompression warnings, this all looks pretty standard. I get my feet under me and pick a direction. The corridors are too small to fly down so I walk with my sword out in front of me.

Their network is incredibly sophisticated. As I attempt to crack it, algorithms shift to compensate. I cannot be certain, but I think they have an AI defending it.

"Take no chances, I don't want someone overriding you and taking over the suit. I don't care how much we think it isn't possible."

Understood.

If I were to design a station, I would put the command center in the exact center. It would be the most shielded from radiation and the most likely to survive any accidents. The way the station is set up I'm on one half, I'll call it the bottom half. I need to go in and up.

The hallway doesn't go far before I run into a closed door marked 'Cargo One'. I put my palm on the panel next to it. Epic overrides it locally in a few seconds and the door hums as it lifts into the ceiling. A large open area stretches out but I don't see any exits to the outside. It has to be the internal bay, like a warehouse distributing the cargo.

There are several fuel lines running through here. Severing them would lead to the station's demise.

"I need him alive, Epic. It's the only way to have my parents back. I'd love to just blow the place up and move on but we can't do that. We need him and a shuttle of some kind or escape pod to return to Earth."

Understood.

I sense more than see movement and turn just as a massive crate crashes down. The metal box slams me hard to the floor. If not for the sword's kinetic emitters I wouldn't have been able to hold onto it. I shove the box off with a growl as a giant, mechanical foot flattens me to the deck. The foot belongs to a huge mech. It has legs like a chicken and a cockpit with tinted glass. Where there should be wings, two armatures extend with grappling claws for cargo.

Amelia, it is exerting tremendous weight, the kinetic emitters are close to maximum.

I fire off the IP cannons in my left hand, hoping to overload the electronics. The blue bolts travel up and down the leg but dissipate before causing any real harm. Alarms flash to life on the HUD letting me know tolerances are approaching maximum.

"Full power to the Emdrive!"

There's a great screeching of metal on metal as thrusters kick in. The mech wobbles as I shoot out from underneath it, leaving a furrow in the metal floor before crashing headlong into a stack of crates.

"IP cannons, narrow beam," I regain my footing, holding my free hand out to fire. The narrow beam intensifies the point of impact. Generally, it makes a target hard to hit, but this thing is fifteen feet tall if it's an inch. The sandpaper staccato rips through the air as I set it to continuous beam. Thankfully, the IP cannons generate next to no heat. They just aren't that effective against shielded things.

Massive clawed arms swipe at me. The sword sparks as I swing it through the joint, severing the limb and sending the chicken-mech scrambling to regain footing.

"All my advanced tech and I'm sword fighting."

There is some irony in this.

"Shut it."

I charge forward, kick in the jets and leap up. The mech swipes at me but I dodge and bring the sword down just behind the cockpit where I think the batteries are. The thing slumps over with a whir of discharging energy and drained solenoids.

There is a panel to your right. Make contact.

The suit clatters against the floor as I run over and slide to a halt, slamming my hand against the control panel.

This is a direct conduit. Shutting down all escape means. No lifepods, no shuttles. There are approximately three hundred individuals on this station, Amelia. We're going to have to do something about them.

"I'll let the government worry about that, our problem is Ericsson."

Each crew member has a RFID tag that shows their clearance and position. I have located Ericsson. Take the third door on the north wall.

I don't know why I thought his door would be more ornate. Instead, it's just another plain, bulkhead door with the plethora of warnings about death and mangled limbs.

"Can you access it?"

As long as their defending AI cannot override direct access, yes I can. It may become aware of the flaw in security shortly.

"Never plug in an unknown computer on your network, right? Okay, do it."

With my palm flat against the interface, Epic overrides the door. It slides up with the same dull hum as the other doors. Inside is a spacious room with a giant picture-window facing the Earth. Reflected sunlight streams in, illuminating the area. Sword out and IP cannons fully charged, I walk in. The other side of the room is living quarters with a bed, desk, and what I presume is the bathroom. This would all be perfectly normal if it weren't for the three men, all in their twenties, sitting blank-eyed and still on the far side. Life signs pop up on the HUD and they all appear normal, except for the lack of brain activity.

"What's wrong with them?"

I think they are in a vegetative state. I am cross-referencing their faces with... yes, they are in the recovered database. All three are or were students at the academy.

"Hello?" I say over the PA. No response. Sensors at full power along with ECM and everything else still working I enter the room, sweeping from side to side. "I thought you said—" The sound of a toilet flushing catches my attention as a man walks out of the bathroom. He smiles at me as he crosses the room to wash his hands.

"Are you Ericsson?"

He chuckles, "That is a name I haven't heard in a long time. Yes, my dear Amelia, I am... or was... Harold Ericsson. You've come a long way to confirm who I am. Is that all you wanted? There are easier—"

"Shut up and stop pretending to be some effete jerk who still thinks he's won. You've lost. It's over. Your coup failed, your company is in tatters and as soon as the UN finds out about this place it will be destroyed. Spare me your idiotic assumptions that you can somehow still defeat me. Got it?"

His smile vanishes and I can see anger in those blue eyes. A light on my HUD catches my attention, the ECM master alarm is flashing. Something is interacting

264

with it. The metallic ink I sprayed over my suit lights up like a diamond under a spotlight. I close my eyes for just a second as fear spikes through me. I hope I did this right...

I open one eye.

"Epic, am I still me?"

I have not detected any change in your brain waves nor has any abnormal energy penetrated the suits shielding.

I let out a huge sigh.

"Impressive," he growls, "You found a way to block telepathy?"

"Are you stupid? Of course I did. You mind-controlled my parents, you mind control telepaths and you think I'm going to walk up here and not be ready for it?" I'm sick of this. I march toward him. I can just stun him and take him back to Earth.

His eyes narrow as I come for him. In a flash he whips out a semi-auto pistol Epic identifies as a Colt 1911A1.

"You can't hurt me with that."

"I can hurt them." He fires a shot. The gun bucks in his hand. My sound system protects my ears but it leaves me deaf for a heartbeat. The closest of the three men slump over, not even registering he's been shot.

Blood seeps out of his chest as his heart continues to beat.

"Bastard," I spit.

"Come any closer and I'll shoot another one."

I freeze. Let him think he has me for a second while he talks.

"You didn't come up here to put me in jail, Ms. Lockheart. What do you want?"

"I would think it was obvious. I want you to fix my parents."

He smiles like a used car salesmen who is about to take some schmucks last dime.

"Of course, why didn't you just ask? I'll happily do this for you if in turn, you show my scientist how to make your armor... and of course, leave here without me."

I shake my head, "That isn't happening and you know it."

"It's your choice. You might be able to stun me before I kill another person, but know this—I will never. Ever. Undo what I did to your parents. You've cost me a hundred years of planning and probably doomed our planet in the process. You think you're the hero with your righteous crusade to free your parents?" He laughs, waving the gun around.

I need to know what he knows and it is clear he is willing to talk about it.

"You're the second person to tell me that. What do you know that I don't?"

"Volumes." I walked into that one. Idiot.

"You know what I mean. The Protector, before your lapdog killed him, told me the same thing. What is going on here?"

He cocks his head to the side I can see him thinking.

"I'll make you a deal, Ms. Lockheart. I will tell you what I know about this. If you will listen and understand. I don't think you can... but... if you truly can understand then maybe we can salvage this situation and save the human race. Deal?"

I hate this smug jerk more every second but the more info I have the better. "Deal."

He lowers his pistol and I lower my sword. I try hard not to think about the dead man laying ten feet away. The man whose whole life was stolen by this jackass.

"Good. I know you're smart, you must have realized by now what I've achieved is beyond human means?"

I nod. We suspected alien but to hear it's confirmation at least

"I was born the moment Tesla threw the switch on his Wardenclyffe tower experiment. The first baby born when extra-dimensional energy poured through our world. I didn't know it then, but I was also the first child born with a superpower. As time went on and I continued to... live... I noticed a pattern to things. War hate, murder, all of it committed in mass scale by the very people we elected to lead us. Do you know the problem with all governments?"

"Usually they're given too much power and allowed to run unchecked."

"Close," he says. He turns around and pulls out a small decanter, pouring himself a drink, he takes a sip before continuing. "Not too much power, not enough. But, if you give a man ultimate power he has such a short time to implement he scrambles and destroys everything. I am effectively immortal. I want what is best for mankind and I have the power to ensure those around me are loyal. I am the perfect tyrant, in the Greek sense of the word."

"The Greeks elected Tyrants when their city-states were out of control. We're hardly out of control."

"You're short-sighted then. I see a world divided by petty differences. Why is it you were ordered to stand down on the Mexican border? What moral right did they have to stop you from saving lives just because of an imaginary line on a map?

"I tell you, none! I want to craft a world with a unified purpose. And believe me, we need it. War is coming. A war like none other and if we aren't unified as a people we will be destroyed. This is what you've upset. This is what you've ruined. Unless you help me rebuild, we'll never be ready."

"Epic, can we break the encryption on this jar of pickles and steal all his info?"

No. Even if I could defeat the AI it would likely delete everything in a last ditch effort to keep us from having it. I predict only a twenty-three percent chance of victory. I cannot recommend that course of action.

"Discussing it with your AI? I have to say, I'm incredibly impressed. It took your mom seven years of eighteen-hour days to develop the coding language and hardware specifications to make an AI."

It took me seven years too, the only difference is I was six when I had the idea. Anger flares up in me and I want to smash this jerk to a pulp.

"Don't talk about my parents. Did it ever occur to you that if you'd come out of the shadows, tried to help us instead of controlling us we might have all achieved together what you tried to take by force?"

"Why do you think I made Cat-7? I wanted to unite the superpowered people under one cause. But as soon as power was on the table, the government tried to take it. No, little girl, after a hundred years I can tell you what people will do before they even know themselves. Recruiting telepaths was my last ditch plan to rule from within the system. Now, all I have left is to make a new system, one that I rule utterly and completely, for our own safety and future."

His points sound reasonable and valid, but so did Stalin's. "Neither you or Pythia, are gods. You don't get to say what's best for anyone. We decide that. You're done, Ericsson. Finished, you can live the rest of your so-called immortal life in prison. We will stand together and win, or we'll lose, but we will do it as a free people. As old as you are I would think you would've studied more history... 'They that can give up essential liberty to obtain a little temporary safety deserve neither liberty nor safety.' You know who said that?"

"A stupid, short-sighted fool who couldn't imagine global extinction. Don't quote Benjamin Franklin to me. You've made your choice then, have you? Think you're simply going to frog march me to a shuttle and take me to Earth?"

"That is exactly the plan." I leap forward with an assist from the Emdrive. I ignore his feeble attempt to bring his weapon up since he can't hurt me and I'm between him and his pets. The gun explodes in fire. He staggers back from the wound, blood flowing from his mouth. I freeze. Shock or horror I'm not sure which. Why would he kill himself?

"What?"

The voice startles me and I spin around, half jumping. The middle man, covered in blood from the dead guy next to him, stands, looking down at his hands.

"How?"

"It's okay you've been—"

"No you twit, how come I'm not you?"

Then it dawns on me why there are so many missing people. So many gaps and different names but the same signature... he isn't immortal.

Amelia. I think he means to transfer himself into you. If not for the ECM it would have likely worked.

"No matter, I shall simply try again." He leaps past me, slides on the floor. I scramble to catch him but before I can he sticks the gun in his mouth and pulls the trigger.

"Dammit!" The third and last man stands. I shake off the shock and cover him with the IP cannon. "You move and I will stun the crap out of you."

"So? What are you going to do Ms. Lockheart? Surely even you must see by now that no prison can contain me. When I die, every time I die, my consciousness is transferred to the nearest individual. It is why I keep so many people around. Please, by all means, take me to Earth. I need to start over anyway and this won't do."

Amelia, we cannot let him return to Earth.

"We can't let him live either, there has to be a way. Scan the room... does he have any orbital controls here?"

His panel appears to have all the master controls for the satellite.

"I know you're trying to figure out how to beat me, but you can't. I've had a hundred years to plan for this moment. Even if you crashed the satellite and killed everyone on board... I'd still live. You can't win, dear. Do you see now why you must join me? Only can lead us through the blight that is coming. When they come, and they will come, if our planet isn't united under one strong leader, all will be lost."

Ignoring him, I find the controls and fire up the panel. I put the sword away so I can have a free hand. The panel lights up and after a quick status check comes back one-hundred percent. I flip through the menus looking for what I want.

Amelia... what about the other people on board?

"Access the PA." I make sure to cover Ericsson so he doesn't move.

Access granted.

"Attention all personnel, this is Arsenal speaking. You have five minutes to abandon ship. The clock is ticking." I hit the klaxon. Alarms ring and a computerized voice says: *All hands abandon station. All hands abandon station.*

"What are you doing?" Ericsson asks me.

I am unlocking the escape pods and shuttle bays for the crew.

"Epic, can you lock out the AI from here?"

Affirmative. He does not appear to have full access beyond his security protocols. While he is excellent at his job he is not allowed outside the one function; Network security. Mr. Ericsson, however, has given this panel full control. Probably under the assumption that he would be the only one who could use it.

"Lock him out of the entire system. I don't want him to have access to anything anywhere on the station, other than food."

What are you doing?" Ericsson shouts, stepping forward with his hands balled into fists. "You can't win. Surely you see that?" *Is that desperation I hear in his voice? The outside of my suit sparkles under his renewed assault.*

The station shudders as a hundred escape pods launch from it like bullets from a gun. I watch the counter go down to zero.

All pods away. He is the only remaining person on the station.

"If you knew me at all, if you knew my parents at all, you would know one thing about me."

"Oh please, spare me your desperate attempt at bravado. If not today, then one day I will show up and you will be bound in your chair and on that day you will lose. For I will become you. Ultimately you cannot win."

I reach over and activate the orbital maneuvering system. The station shudders again, this time it doesn't stop as all the jets facing 'west' go into full burn, increasing the orbital speed of the station.

"When I was a child I was told my parents were dead. I was told I would never walk again. I was told I couldn't make an AI and I was told my suit would never work. I was told I would lose." I move around the console, leaving one hand on it long enough for Epic to lock in my instructions and then lockout the console.

"I overcame all of that, you know why?"

"Because of your pluck and persistence? I clearly will not make the mistake of—"

"No, Ericsson. I'm here because I don't believe in the 'no-win' scenario."

His eyes go wide and I trigger my IP cannons.

27

"How do you know he's still up there?" Luke asks as we snuggle under a white goose down comforter. He's letting me stay with him until I can find a new place to live. I gave the house away to Carlos' older brother, whose family needed a place. I used a phony contest so he wouldn't feel any shame in accepting such a gift. Since I flattened the HQ, well technically more than flattened, I'm homeless.

"Epic rigged one of the cameras we found to keep an eye on him."

"But how did you keep him there? I know you don't have a lot of manual dexterity when you're in the armor."

I smile as he pulls me tight, running his big hands through my hair. God, I needed this. "The station had living quarters for three hundred people, I just piled every mattress I could find on top of him

When I left I had fifty pushed into the room, I could barely shut the door."

"You're kidding me," he says as he kisses my neck.

I practically purr, "Nope. Epic wanted me to break his arms and legs but I'm not Prince Humperdinck—"

"Who?"

"You didn't just say that," I sigh. "How has your film education been so neglected?"

He nibbles my ear and thoughts of movies go right out the window.

The last few days have been interesting in the Chinese sense of the word. By order of the Federal government, all state militias were disbanded in favor of national teams. I guess Ericsson got his wish after all. A thought that runs shivers up my spine. They will still be based on region but they will have more members, better training, and FBI-like authority. The one caveat to state's rights is the governors of the regional areas they are based out of can deploy the teams as needed.

Three days after I returned home the station passed through the Van Allen belt, the ultimate

Faraday Cage ensuring Ericsson can never return to Earth.

A knock on the front door interrupts hi exploring of my neck. With a sigh, he drags himself ou of bed. I roll over to watch the ripple of muscles up and down his back and legs as he slides on jeans. I still have a lot to think about. What's next? It doesn't take him long to answer the door and I hear him say my name "Amelia, it's for you."

The only people who even know I'm here woul call first before coming over and Kate's already visited Not that she would use the door. It's like she has a allergy to them or something.

"Whoever it is, tell them to go away."

"You really need to come out here. Want me t come help?"

I growl as I toss the covers back. This better b worth it. I'm a pro at getting in and out of my chair s it only takes me a few seconds to slide in then pull shirt over my tank top. I grab my breakfast on the wa out, a half-eaten PB&J Luke made me an hour before.

I freeze half way in the living room. I've only eve seen the man standing in the door on TV, not i person. The President's blue suit is impeccab tailored. As he shakes Luke's hand I can tell the ma spends time in the gym, fabric pulls around his shoulders the same way Luke's does. Two men flank him, one of whom I recognize from the White House battle.

He smiles to Luke before turning his brown eyes on me. "May I come in?" The President asks casually.

"Of course sir, yes sir," Luke spits out rapidly.

The President flashes Luke an amused, but grateful grin as he walks in. The two secret service men follow him in and check out the apartment for a second.

"Luke, manners," I say to kickstart him.

"Right! Sir, please have a seat. Can I get you anything to eat or drink?" Poor Luke is speaking so fast I can barely understand him.

"Thank you, son, no I'm good. I'm afraid I can't stay long, though. May I have a moment with Ms. Lockheart?"

Cautiously I reach into the pouch on the side of my chair and retrieve my glasses. I don't need them to see, they're my link to Epic. The chair I'm in is nothing more than a normal chair. My Mark II is done for and we're going to need to start working on a Mark III.

He's older than he looks on TV, I guess they probably try hard to make him look young. I can only imagine how he feels leading the country. The last few weeks have aged the crap out of me. I keep expecting to find a grey hair when I look in the mirror. Twenty-One is only a month away so why do I feel twice that age?

He waits patiently for Luke to leave the room before holding his hand out to me.

"Thank you, for what you did. Your country owes you a debt of gratitude." I purse my lips together desperate not to blush. "I don't suppose I could ask you to be on any of our teams? You could run it, have the whole thing to do with as you please? Clearly, you can be trusted."

"Mr. President, I thank you for your faith in me sir, but I wasn't being altruistic. I was trying to stop the man who kidnapped my parents and mind-controlled them."

His eyes drop to the floor as he speaks, "I'm aware and I'm very sorry about that. But," he says looking at me, "I don't think you give yourself enough credit. Without the help of you and your... friend... I'd be dead and the country would be no more."

Does he mean me?

"My friend... is he okay to go on? You're not—"

He holds up his hand, "As long as you keep him hidden then we won't have a problem. I have several

nen from cybersecurity who would love to pick his
brain if you would allow it. The ease of which he moves
through our computer systems has given the joint
chiefs a collective heart attack."

"I can imagine. I'll see what I can do. As for the
team... let me think about it."

"Sir, we've got to go," the man from the White
House battle says.

"Is that a no, then?"

"It's a 'let me think about it'," I say with a smile.

"Of course. It was a pleasure miss," he turns to
the man in the corner, "Palmer, give her your card
please." Palmer instantly reaches into his pocket and
retrieves a white card, he leans down to give it to me
and as I catch his eye he mouths, 'thank you'.

I smile back at him, still blushing like mad. I
don't normally talk to people about my activities inside
the armor.

"One more thing. NASA detected a massive
unknown station breaking orbit three days ago. They
have it colliding with the sun in a few years. Would I be
correct in assuming it had the man responsible for all
of this on board?"

I nod. A lump forms in my throat and I can't risk
speaking.

"Good to know. Good day, Ms. Lockheart."

My mind catches up with what is happening and I wheel forward as he leaves, "Sir?"

"Yes?"

"The Protector died defending DC. If there is to be a monument of any kind, I would like it to be of him."

"I'll see what I can do. Take care Ms. Lockheart let me know what you decide." He left in a hurry, his men shutting the door behind him.

Luke rushes in and looks between the door, then me, then back to the door. "Do you know who that was?"

"He's President, Luke, not William Shatner, calm down."

"William... Amelia, you just got a personal visit from the leader of the free world! What did he want?"

"Food first, then politics. Go, pizza, root beer, now!" I smack his tight bottom with my hand. Then I shake it muttering 'ow' over and over. He lets out a big sigh and marches to the kitchen to get his keys.

Why didn't you tell him about the aliens?

"I barely believe myself, I don't think anyone else will. Pythia didn't even see them she just senses their actions."

I smile at Luke as he closes the door, giving me one last peering gaze before shutting it all the way.

What are we going to do then? They are coming and we know nothing about them or how to stop them.

"Ericsson was right about one thing."

What?

"We need unity. We need a team, Epic. We need a solid team if we're going to fight this."

I'll start running numbers on people.

"Good, but I already know at least a few people who are going to be involved. Call Kate, I want to fill her in personally."

Do you think she will believe you?

"At least she won't think I'm making it up," I tell him. I run my hands through my hair and shake my head back-and-forth. I'm not, right? I didn't lose my mind and suddenly see conspiracies where none existed? No. I know what I saw and what I heard.

They're coming. The question is, can we stop them?

THE END.

EPILOGUE

Carlos closed the case on his guitar, shoving it int the corner to rest on a pile of dirty clothes. H didn't want to do laundry and he was too worried t play.

Three days since he saw her on the news fightin that monstrosity in DC. Three days. Not a word the suddenly this morning he gets an email from Ep letting him know she was alright.

He kicked a pillow across the room. He'd felt s helpless watching her. Not for the hundredth tim since he met Amelia he wished for powers of his ow That wasn't happening. While he would never tell he he'd taken the test twice. He was so sure it had bee wrong the first time.

With an exasperated sigh, he slunk onto the bed. There was no hope. He saw her less and less every week and now she couldn't even let him know in person she was alive. Part of him, the more reasonable part, understood. But for six years he had her all to himself, and yeah, he knew there was nothing romantic between them, but she was his best friend. And he missed her.

"No hope at all," he muttered.

He was trapped between going downstairs and looking for food or staying up all night playing Xbox without it. If he went downstairs he'd have to face his parents. He really could do without another lecture about his future. He had to have an old bag of chips up here somewhere? The TV powered on with a flash of light blinding him.

"What the?" He grabbed the remote and mashed the button until the TV turned off. The light didn't go away. It was coming from the closet. Every scary movie he'd ever seen ran through his mind. He backed away from the glowing door holding his controller above his head as a weapon.

The door opened. A girl, not even a ghostly girl, just a girl in a white gown with a crown of lavender flowers around her head and long black hair and big blue eyes. Carlos blinked several times. She couldn't be more than thirteen, though something about her seemed far older.

"Uh, hi?"

"Hello, Carlos. Your destiny awaits."

From The Author

There it is, aliens! I hope you enjoyed the heck out of book two. I sure had a blast writing it. I want to say a big 'thank you' to everyone who's made it this far. You are directly responsible for me living my dream! Amazon is terrible at letting you know when my next book is out, sign up for the earliest notification (www.jefferyhhaskell.com) Or, if you prefer Facebook (I know I do) then find me at https://www.facebook.com/jefferyhhaskell/ Signing up has its privileges. I have free stories, giveaways and tons of insider info on my process and what I'm working on. I love talking to fans so come by and say hi!

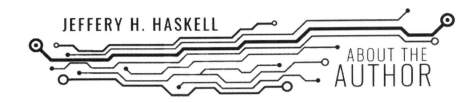

JEFFERY H. HASKELL

ABOUT THE AUTHOR

Husband, father, writer, in that order. Jeff love sharing his vision of military sci-fi and superheroe with anyone who will sit still long enough. Read h other works on Amazon.com

93755130R00173

Made in the USA
Lexington, KY
17 July 2018